THE HEART OF A MAN

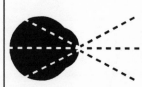

This Large Print Book carries the
Seal of Approval of N.A.V.H.

THE HEART OF A MAN

DEB KASTNER

THORNDIKE PRESS

An imprint of Thomson Gale, a part of The Thomson Corporation

Detroit • New York • San Francisco • New Haven, Conn. • Waterville, Maine • London

THOMSON

GALE

LIBRARY OF CONGRESS CATALOGING-IN-PUBLICATION DATA

Kastner, Debra.
   The heart of a man / by Deb Kastner.
     p. cm. — (Thorndike Press large print Christian fiction)
     ISBN 0-7862-9164-8 (lg. print : alk. paper) 1. Large type books. I. Title.
   PS3561.A724H43 2006
   813'.54—dc22
                                               2006026741

U.S. Hardcover:
ISBN 13: 978-0-7862-9164-9
ISBN 10: 0-7862-9164-8

Published in 2006 by arrangement with Harlequin Books S.A.

Printed in the United States of America on permanent paper
10 9 8 7 6 5 4 3 2 1

Then Moses said to the Lord, "O my Lord, I am not eloquent, neither before nor since You have spoken to Your servant; but I am slow of speech and slow of tongue." So the Lord said to him, "Who has made man's mouth? Or who makes the mute, the deaf, the seeing, or the blind? Have not I, the Lord? Now therefore, go, and I will be with your mouth and teach you what you shall say."

— *Exodus* 4:10–12

To my sweet middle girl, Kimmi, who is the absolute last word on fashion in our house. This incredibly talented girl can make anything with a piece of fabric and some thread. My own personal image consultant, she continues to remind me fashion can be comfortable, just as I continue to break that rule by wearing sweats when I write.

Much thanks and gratitude to my oldest daughter, Annie, who transcribed much of this book for me onto the computer, as I am one of those dinosaurs who still prefer to create in longhand.

CHAPTER ONE

"How do you do that?"

The question came from her best friend since childhood, Camille O'Shay. They had grown up together in a tiny rural Texas town, attended the same college and now were sharing living quarters in the heart of downtown Denver.

"Do what, Millie?" she asked absently, her eyes carefully scrutinizing the gentleman under her authority, her eyes taking in every seam and pleat as she tucked and pinned.

"Completely change people's appearances, Izzy, like someone's fairy godmother or something," Camille said with a laugh. "I'm completely astounded by your ability to wave your wand and work wonders."

Isobel Buckley shrugged. "It's my job to dress and press these gorgeous gals and pretty boys and get them looking their best for the boardroom. The final product depends on me. It's hard work, not waving wands, that yields a final product I can be satisfied with."

She wasn't telling her friend any new information — Camille was well familiar that Isobel was a personal shopper and image consultant for a select, high-end clientele. And Camille likewise knew Isobel was every bit the perfectionist she sounded.

"You know, when you think about it, it doesn't really take much to make high-quality fashion look good on those pinup model hunks you work with," Camille observed wryly. "Although, of course, dear heart, you do it better than most."

"What's that supposed to mean?" Isobel was busy straightening a silk tie on one of those so-called pinup model hunks who wanted to look his best for a national conference, and was only half paying attention to her friend's happy chatter.

"Turn around for me," she told the man, who willingly complied.

"Oh, nothing," Camille replied, not sounding the least bit convinced as Isobel turned her attention back to her friend for a moment. "I was just wondering if you could do the same kind of work with an *average* man, someone who hasn't ever read a men's fashion magazine."

"What are you talking about?" Isobel said,

throwing a quick glance in Camille's direction. "You're babbling nonsense."

"Am I?" she shot back, her grin reminding Isobel of a cat crouched to pounce on a helpless mouse. "What do you think about adding a run-of-the-mill variety guy to your clientele? The kind of guy *I* usually date, as opposed to the kind of guy you *could* date if you weren't so caught up in your career?"

Isobel rolled her eyes. "I'm going to pretend you didn't say that."

"So are you up for it?" Camille actually sounded excited, as if she were taking the idea for real.

"I beg your pardon?"

"Making a normal slob of a guy into *Mr. Right*. Blue-collar material, ya know? It would be fun."

Camille was definitely warming up to the idea, while Isobel was beginning to cringe. Her friend was sounding all too serious about this fanatical, half-baked scheme.

"Here's what we'll do. I'll pick the guy, and you'll have six weeks to make him into a real man. The man of every girl's dreams."

"You're kidding, right?" Isobel took a deep breath and held it. She could only hope.

Camille shrugged, a noncommittal gesture. "Maybe. Maybe not. But don't be surprised if I come knocking on your door with a fellow who desperately needs your help for a makeover."

Isobel pinched her lips, deciding to ignore her friend's obviously off-the-top-of-her-head twaddle. It would come to nothing in the long run.

She hoped.

Not more than two days later, her dear childhood confidante made good on her threat. Bursting into Isobel's office, Camille announced in a loud, triumphant voice, "I've found him!"

"I'm sorry," Isobel said, distracted by the pile of paperwork she was muddling through, piece by agonizingly slow piece. "You found whom?"

"The guy, of course. The one you're going to wave your magic wand over." She looked disappointed for a moment. "Our average guy, remember?"

Isobel smoothed her thick, long brown hair with her palm and sighed, desperately wishing she *didn't* remember. "I would ask if you were joking, but I know you better than that. What possessed you to go through with this crazy scheme? This isn't even remotely close to real life, Camille."

"I wasn't even looking! I'm telling you the truth. No one could have been more shocked or amazed than I. All I was doing was talking with a regular patron at my hotel — a *rich,* quite handsome, very well-connected patron, I might add."

"All the people who spend time at your hotel are rich," Isobel reminded her friend blithely. "And well-connected. Handsome, though. Since when is that a requirement for hotel patronage?" she teased.

"Oh, Isobel. You have no idea. This guy is out of this world!" She stopped suddenly and clapped a hand over her heart, sighing loudly and dramatically, even as a dark blush stole up her cheeks. "Addison Fairfax."

"But that's not the point." She faltered for a moment, and Isobel found a bit of humor in the fact that her dear friend was actually flustered over this *Addison Fairfax.* It took a lot for Camille to show interest in a particular man, preferring in general the whole of mankind.

"Go ahead, Camille," Isobel encouraged with a smile and a sly wink that let her friend know she was on to her. "Handsome and . . . ?"

Camille placed a hand on her reddened cheek and continued. "We were making our usual small talk, you know, and I was telling him about my brilliant idea for you to make over some regular guy — not anything like Addison, of course. He dresses divinely."

She followed her high-speed discourse with another long, drawn-out sigh.

Isobel chuckled.

"Well, the next thing you know, he's telling me all about his problems. You are the answer to his prayers, Isobel, I kid you not. Neither of us could believe it!"

"I might as well hear it," Isobel said with a groan. "Go on."

"Okay, I'll tell you," she agreed, casually stringing it on with a laugh. "But Izzy, you have to promise to listen all the way through before you jump to any conclusions."

Isobel smiled. She was certain she'd be *jumping to conclusions* long before her friend was finished telling what was sure to be a wildly fantastical story — but she *could* promise to keep her thoughts to herself, at least until she'd sorted the whole wild, bizarre idea out in her mind.

"So, it's like this," Camille began with a flourish of her hand.

"Once upon a time," Isobel teased.

Camille threw her a mock glare. "If you're going to keep interrupting every time I speak, I'm never going to get through this."

Isobel chuckled. "Sorry. It won't happen again." She made the motion of zipping her lips closed with her thumb and index finger.

"So there's this man I was telling you about, Addison Fairfax, who often uses our hotel for his meetings and conventions," Camille said, her voice growing with excitement at every word. "He's the CEO of Security, Inc. You know it?"

"I've heard of it," Isobel replied. Of course she knew the name. It was only one of the most prestigious financial firms in Denver, probably on the continent.

Everyone had *heard* of Security, Inc.

"You can only imagine how successful Addison is, not to mention how wonderfully handsome he looks. He's always polished, precise and dressed meticulously."

"So, what's the problem?" Isobel asked, wondering how she could help such a high-and-mighty being, and why on earth he would think to pay her for it. Sounded to her as if he had it made.

Unless, like many of her clientele, he was simply too busy to worry about fashion. But then, where would be the challenge in that? He was the type of man Isobel worked with on a regular basis in her business, not something out of her league.

"Oh, it's not Addison," Camille said, holding her hands up, palms out. "You can trust me on this. That man is perfect just the way he is."

Isobel laughed. "It sounds as if you have a genuine, fully loaded crush on the man."

"A *crush?*" Her friend sounded mortified. "I would never stoop so low. I haven't had a crush on a man since ninth grade." She sniffed, her nose in the air like a cat who'd been offended.

"Tenth grade. Mr. Monahue, our history teacher," Isobel reminded her with a smile.

Camille chuckled. "Oh, he was cute, wasn't he? If I recall, I wasn't the only one who thought he floated over the ground."

Isobel shook her head, smiling at the memory. *Every* tenth-grade girl in Mr. Monahue's class had had a crush on the charming teacher.

She shook her head again, her mind returning to the present dilemma. "Okay, so Addison Fairfax is *interesting,*" she said, rephrasing for her friend's sake and to keep the conversation on line. "But I still don't understand what that has to do with me."

"It's his younger brother, Dustin. Now, Dustin is a mess — a regular slob, in Addison's words. And Addison actually wants to *pay* you to whip him into shape. Six short weeks of work and an enormous salary tacked on as a bonus. Think of it, Isobel!

16

You don't even have to stop your own work to help him."

"Why would I want to do this, again?" Isobel asked, crossing her arms and tipping her executive-style black leather chair as far back as it would go, wishing for a short moment it would crash backward, sending her down through the twenty-two floors below and away from her glassy-eyed friend and the half-cocked ideas spouting from her lips.

"Remember our conversation from the other day?" Camille reminded her, dangling the thought out before her like a carrot to a rabbit.

"I remember *you* saying a bunch of stuff. I don't remember *me* saying anything at all. Most particularly that I wanted to participate in such nonsense."

"Oh, but you do, Isobel, whether you want to admit it now or not. Think of the tremendous challenge involved. I know you love the idea, deep down. Admit it!"

Isobel crossed her arms and shook her head. Vehemently.

"Don't you see? Dustin Fairfax would be a test of your true strength as an image consultant." Camille raised her hands to emphasize the mental marquee board. "I mean, they make gorgeous hunks into ugly bums all the time in the movies. Don't you

17

think you could do the opposite for one poor man who needs what only your special brand of fashion sense can bring to him? He'll be a new man!"

Isobel admitted — in her heart, anyway — that she was intrigued, despite every bone of sense in her body screaming to the contrary. Something about the whole setup just didn't seem right, though she wasn't sure what was bothering her.

It sounded innocent enough on the outside, but something . . .

"How old is this man?" she asked after a slight but pregnant pause.

"Dustin?" Camille asked, her eyes gleaming with the victory she sensed was coming.

Isobel was quite aware Camille knew her better than anyone. They'd spent their whole lives together, been best friends forever. Camille would know that once Isobel capitulated in the least, she had her bagged and roasted for sure.

Camille certainly looked like a tiger hunter in full triumph, stripes sighted down her scope.

"Well, I know Addison is thirty-three," her friend supplied thoughtfully. "And since Dustin is his younger brother, I would guess he'd be about thirty, give or take a year."

"And what, exactly, is wrong with him?"

she asked, feeling as if she ought to be taking notes. "I have to know the truth, here, if you want me to help."

"Oh, nothing's wrong with him, really," Camille exclaimed with a high laugh. "Addison said he's just — flighty. That's the word he used."

Isobel raised one eyebrow. Here, she suspected, was where the roof caved in.

"At least by Addison's standards, Dustin doesn't dress very well. He's not sophisticated. That shouldn't be a huge challenge for you."

"He's not a homeless man or something like that?" Isobel was still cautious. Too much about this story still didn't mesh. Something was off just a little, though she couldn't put her finger on just what it was.

She gave Camille a hard, serious stare. "Dustin is aware this is going to happen to him? He has agreed to work with me?"

"He happens to own a small flower store on the 16th Street Mall. Retail, you know? He's successful, in his own way, I guess, though he's a long way from the clientele you're used to working with."

Camille paused, running her tongue along her bottom lip. "And as for your other question, he hasn't exactly been told. Yet."

Isobel opened her mouth to argue but

Camille held her hands up to cut her off.

"As soon as you agree, Addison will make sure Dustin knows to expect you. It's all been arranged, but Addison didn't want to speak to his brother about it until I'd finalized things with you."

"What if Dustin says no?"

"He won't," Camille said with a firm nod. "He might want to, but he won't. You see, there's money riding on this venture. Apparently quite a lot of money."

"He will get a lot of money if he learns to dress well?" Isobel asked, stymied. "But deep down he really wouldn't want to do this. Is that what you're really telling me?"

"It's complicated," Camille explained with a patient sigh. "Addison was left to execute his father's will, and Izzy, the poor man is beside himself, with the situation being what it is. I feel so sorry for him. What a predicament!"

"Go on," Isobel urged, not at all certain she wanted to hear more.

"Apparently their father was afraid Dustin would squander his inheritance away instead of doing something useful with it. Addison is terribly worried about his brother. I guess he's kind of stubborn, and he's definitely his own man. Marches to the beat of his own drummer, so to speak."

20

She paused, clasping her hand over her heart in the melodramatic way that was uniquely Camille's. "Can you imagine the tremendously heavy burden their father left on poor Addison?"

"How so?"

"Addison was named Dustin's trustee in the will, even though Dustin is a full-grown man. You can imagine how *Dustin* felt. And Addison certainly didn't ask for the formidable task of bringing Dustin into line. According to the terms of the will, Dustin has certain obligations to meet — delineated by his father — in order for Addison to release the funds to his brother."

"He has to learn to dress well?" Isobel asked again, befuddled. "In order to get his hands on his rightful inheritance?"

None of this made the least bit of sense, and Isobel was beginning to feel very much as if she'd stepped into another dimension.

What kind of a man was Dustin, that his father would put such insane demands on him?

One thing she knew for certain — *she* would balk at such radical and unusual demands being placed upon her. If Dustin were *half* the independent spirit Camille had described him to be . . .

Camille laughed. "No, of course not, silly.

He has to make a splash in society or something outrageous like that, and of course clothes make the man, right?"

"It's a good start," Isobel said with a laugh and a shrug. *I'd be looking for a little more than that in a man.*

Camille giggled. "After I told Addison about you, he thought you'd be the perfect person to bring Dustin around. You, of all people, can guide him in making a true contribution to society. Those are the exact terms of the will. Can you believe it?"

"I see," Isobel said under her breath, though she wasn't sure she did. The idea was intriguing, of course; definitely intriguing. The thought of transforming a scalawag of a man into a prince would be a challenge, but it also sounded kind of fun.

"Okay," she said after only a brief pause to consider the short- and long-term ramifications of her decision. She didn't want to examine her own motives too closely. "I'll do it."

She didn't ask how much money she would make. She was taking on this *project* for the challenge, and she trusted Camille that the time she spent would be worth her weight in gold. Literally.

And she was surprised by how excited she was at the prospect of making over the erstwhile Dustin. It had been a long time since she'd done something truly stimulating, and her heart was pounding with anticipation.

"I knew this was something you'd want to do," Camille squealed, throwing her arms around Isobel's neck and dancing her around in dizzying circles. "Oh, how wonderful for you!"

"Wonderful for *me?*" she asked, laughing at her friend's excited antics. "I thought Dustin was the one to benefit from this deal."

"Oh, he will," her friend agreed immediately. "He most definitely will. But won't it be such fun for you, as well? Admit it. You love the idea. *Pygmalion* at its best."

"I suppose the idea has merit," she agreed. "I do have one condition, however, and I refuse to take on this *project* unless it is met unconditionally."

"What's that?"

"This Dustin guy — he has to go into this experiment with his eyes wide open. If he doesn't agree to the makeover, if he is not comfortable with the idea of working with me or if he expresses doubts or disinterest, I do not want to move forward with this." Isobel listed items on her fingers. "The project must all be conducted on the up-

and-up, with everything laid out up front for Dustin and for me. No surprises and no reluctant subjects. Do you understand what I'm getting at here?"

"I'll speak to Addison immediately," Camille assured her, obviously trying to rein in her high, excited tone and appear more businesslike and reserved. It didn't fool Isobel for a moment.

Her friend continued, gulping in air to remain calm. "He said he would be the one to speak to Dustin about it and firm up the final details. After that I'll be able to let you know when and where you two can meet and get the ball rolling toward Dustin's new look. He's got to agree. He just has to." She winked. "Especially when he meets *you.*"

"What's that supposed to mean?" Isobel squawked, feigning offense and pressing her lips together to keep her smile hidden.

"Why, you're so pretty you'll knock his socks off. And then, my dear friend, you can replace them with preppie argyles."

"Oh, I just love it when I get to play fairy godmother," Isobel teased, waving an invisible magic wand through the air. "But this sounds just a little too weird to be real."

Camille laughed and whirled about on her toes like a ballerina. So much for her businesslike demeanor, Isobel thought, smothering her grin. She didn't know where her friend got all her energy, but she wished just a little of it would rub off on her.

"There's a first time for everything, Izzy," Camille said, clapping her hands in anticipation. "And you, my dearest friend in all the world, are going to be the best thing that ever happened to Dustin Fairfax. He won't even know what hit him."

CHAPTER TWO

Dustin lifted the drumsticks into the air, adjusting his grip on the wood so he could play the drum set that curved around the stool on which he sat. He closed his eyes and with a flick of one drumstick, adjusted his backward black-and-purple Colorado Rockies cap to keep his curly black hair out of his face.

His music of choice, at the moment, anyway, was a trumpet-licking jazz CD he'd picked up over the weekend. Eclectic was the only way to describe his taste — in music, or in anything else he had a strong opinion about.

The drum set was new — or at least, new to him. A friend who had been a drummer in a high-school band was getting rid of it to make room for a baby crib.

Dustin had grabbed the opportunity and bought the set for a song. He'd never played a percussion instrument in his life, but he figured now was as good a time as any to learn.

It wasn't the first instrument he would have taught himself to play in his life.

How hard could it be?

He made a couple of tentative taps on the snare drum with his sticks, and then pounded the bass a few times with the foot pedal.

Smiling with satisfaction, he began pounding in earnest, perfect rhythm with the beat of the jazz CD. He didn't care at the moment whether or not he sounded good. He was only trying to have a good time. Technique would come later, with many strenuous hours of practice, he knew.

He sent a timely prayer to God that the insulation in his house would be sufficient to keep his neighbors from knocking his door down with their complaints about the horrible din.

Suddenly, out of nowhere, someone clamped his hand tightly on Dustin's shoulder.

Dustin made an instinctive move, standing in a flash, turning and knocking the man's hand away in one swift motion of his elbow and then crouching to pounce on the unknown intruder.

"Hey, take it easy," Addison said with a

deep, dry laugh Dustin immediately recognized. "I didn't mean to startle you. I tried knocking, but you couldn't hear me over all that racket. Sounded like the roof was caving in or something."

Dustin chuckled.

Addison shook his head and laughed in tune with his brother. "The door was open, so I just let myself in. I hope you don't mind."

Dustin wiped his arm against his forehead, as his hands were still tightly gripping the drumsticks. "Naw. Guess I was pretty distracted, messing with this thing." He popped a quick beat on the snare drum for emphasis, then clasped both sticks together and jammed them in the back pocket of his jeans.

He crossed his arms over his chest and stared at his suit-clad big brother. "What are you doing here, Addy boy?" he asked in genuine surprise.

Addison rarely visited Dustin's small house, which was located in Wheatridge, one of the many sprawling suburbs of Denver. In fact, he'd never been there without a direct invitation first.

He had shown little interest in Dustin's hobbies, or anything else for that matter. They had never been close, even as children.

Addison was the jock, and Dustin the artist. It had always been that way.

Addison wasn't fond of anything artistic, from drama to Monet. Football, baseball, soccer — these had made up Addison's teenage world.

And Addison had always been the brains in the family, in Dustin's estimation. As the CEO for a major financial corporation, and an important person in the Denver social scene, Addison didn't have time to dabble with anything beyond the walls of his chic, downtown penthouse condo and lush corner office. His only interest in the arts as a successful adult was as his business required, and nothing more.

"I've come about Dad's will, Dustin — specifically, the terms of the trust fund," Addison said tersely and abruptly in the crisp business tone he always used. Dustin sometimes thought Addison hid behind that tone in order to keep his emotions on a back burner. The two brothers certainly weren't as close as Dustin would have liked, though he put the blame for that more on his father than on Addison.

Dustin clasped his hands behind his back. His father's will was not something he really wished to discuss, though he knew it was inevitable. It had to be done, and sooner rather than later. Addison was right on that one point, anyway.

Their mother had died when Dustin was fourteen and Addison was sixteen. He remembered her as a sweet, delicate woman who always smiled and always had an eye and an open hand for the poor and needy. She had kept the house full of laughter and singing, and always had a prayer or a song of praise on her lips.

His father, on the other hand, was as cold as stone, a strict disciplinarian who practiced what he preached — that God helped those who helped themselves.

Never mind that *that* particular "verse" wasn't really in the Bible.

Addison Fairfax, Sr., had worked long hours establishing the firm Addison Jr. now led and held a majority interest in.

Dustin knew his father had wanted him in the company, as well. Addison Sr. had been bitterly disappointed when, as a young man following his own strong, surging creative impulses, Dustin took a different career path.

To Dustin, being boxed up in an office all day would be like caging a wild beast; and the thought of spending all day crunching numbers — especially anything to do with money — made him shiver.

It was enough just to balance his checkbook every month. That was not the kind of life for him, caged behind a desk with nothing but figures on paper for company.

He wanted to help people, but in another, more creative fashion. One on one, where he could reach out and touch his customers, smile and encourage them to smile back at him.

He pinched his lips together to keep his smile hidden from his brother's observant gaze. It was an understatement to say that math had never been one of Dustin's better subjects.

And so now it came down to his father's last wishes, laid out plainly, literally in black and white. Dustin had been at the formal reading of the will. He knew what it contained, especially in regard to what he was expected to accomplish in order to win the coveted trust fund, which Dustin desperately wanted, but for reasons he would disclose to no one.

At least not yet.

And that was no doubt why Addison was visiting him today. It was up to his big brother, as trustee of the fund in Dustin's name, to see that Dustin cleaned up, became a pillar of society and made a *real* contribution to the world in some way not explicitly drawn out in the will, but legal nonetheless.

Dustin knew Addison wasn't thrilled with the job. He had enough responsibility with his own work without burdening himself with his younger brother's supposed faults. But there was one thing Dustin knew about his older brother — he would follow his father's dictates to the letter without question.

Even if Addison didn't necessarily agree with the terms. Besides, it was legal, drawn up and finalized by their father, who'd known exactly what he was doing.

"You want the money, don't you?" Addison asked crisply, his golden-blond eyebrows creasing low in concern over his blue eyes, all traits of his father.

Dustin had his mother's curly black hair and green eyes. It was a startling contrast between the two brothers, and just one more way they were different from one another.

Dustin took a deep, steadying breath. "Yes, I do," he said solemnly. "You know I do."

That was as much information as he was willing to offer, which no doubt perplexed his older brother.

"Hey, Addy boy," he said, cheerfully

changing the subject, "you want a soda or something?"

"I've asked you repeatedly not to call me that," his brother responded through gritted teeth, shaking his head in warning.

"Why do you think I do it?" Dustin responded with a laugh.

"You little punk," Addison said affectionately. He grabbed Dustin around the neck and scrubbed his knuckles across Dustin's scalp, just the sort of roughhousing they'd done as kids. "Don't forget I'm bigger than you. I can still knock your block off anytime I want."

"I'd like to see you try," Dustin challenged, grabbing his brother by the waist in what amounted to a wrestler's hold.

Addison sighed and abruptly released his hold on Dustin. "As much as I'd like to monkey around with you, bro, I just don't have time today. I'm behind on my schedule already just by being here. Can we just get this painful business settled as quickly as possible so I can return to work?"

This business. Was that all it was to Addison? Another piece of business to settle and then move on? It was only Dustin's life they were talking about.

And so much more. If only Addison knew. But Dustin wasn't ready to trust his brother with more information than he'd already given.

Dustin felt like no more than a thorn in Addison's side at times, a trial to be borne through and just as quickly forgotten.

Addison was staring at him. "I'm sorry to say this, little brother, but you need a make-over," he said soberly, though his eyes were gleaming with amusement at the prospect.

Dustin grinned and crossed his arms over his chest in an instinctively protective gesture. "Oh, like a facial and a mud bath, right? You want me to get a manicure and a massage?"

Addison cleared his throat and looked out the nearest window, gazing for some time before speaking. "This is a very serious matter. You joke about everything," he said softly.

Dustin shrugged. "Of course. In my book, it's better to go through life with a smile than to be grouchy all the time."

"Grouchy? Is that how you see me?" He sounded genuinely surprised.

Dustin shook his head. "I was speaking in relative terms."

"Yes, well, I'm not sure I believe you, but let us get back to the subject at hand. As it happens, per the will, I've hired a girl —"

"No way." Dustin cut him off with his

voice, and concurrently made a severe chopping gesture with the flat of his hand. "My personal life is mine. I won't be set up, even by you."

"I'm not talking about your personal life, Dustin," Addison said, sounding as if he were straining to be patient, and yet with the hint of laughter to his voice. "I'm talking about your image. Who you know, where you go and especially how you dress. A change you and I both know would make our father happy."

Dustin looked down at his old tennis shoes, faded blue jeans and worn gray T-shirt. "What's wrong with the way I dress?"

"That's exactly the point, my man. This woman I hired, Isobel Buckley, knows what's in fashion and helps people change their image. She does it for a living, and I'm sure she could advise you better than I. Honestly, baby brother, you don't have a clue. Admit it. You're a world-class chump."

Dustin felt pressure building up in his chest. Addison was forcing his hand, and they both knew it.

And they both knew he would cave, eventually, before it was all said and done.

He *had* to cave. For the sake of the money. There was no other way.

For a moment, he considered tackling his older brother and wrestling him to the ground, as they had often done as youngsters. It would serve his big brother right to give him the good pounding he had threatened and that he was now certain Addison deserved.

With deep restraint he denied the urge, knowing it would do nothing more than prove Addison's point. Bad clothes and bad manners.

A chump.

"Frankly —" Addison continued in his best, solid business voice "— and you know I'm right in saying this, Father was concerned about the way you would spend your inheritance."

Addison paused, leaning one hand against a nearby table and pulling his brown tweed jacket back to put his hand in his slacks pocket.

To Dustin, it was like seeing his father all over again.

"You have no vision, Dustin. You own a small flower shop, you bang like an Aborigine on this drum of yours in the name of *fun,* and that's all you have to show for yourself. For your time. For your life."

"Is that you or Dad talking?" Dustin goaded through clenched teeth.

It wasn't a fair question, and Dustin immediately regretted his hasty query. It was clearly his father's intention to make Dustin into a different man. Addison was merely the messenger.

The urge to pounce on his burly brother and mess up his fancy suit was growing by the moment, but he knew better than to shoot the messenger, no matter how tempting it might be. It wouldn't solve anything in the long run, and he needed access to that trust fund.

"It's *my* life," he complained, sounding as surly as a little boy. "What's wrong with my flower store?"

"Nothing is wrong with your little shop. But have you ever thought about opening up a chain of stores? What about making a real name for yourself in the Denver social scene? Why not cater to a higher-level clientele, boost your own income?

"You spend as much time gallivanting around town, and who knows what else, as you do putting your strength and effort into your business." Addison took an extended breath. "What you need is to go to the right parties and rub elbows with the right people. Build up relationships that mean something. Really make something important of yourself."

Addison rubbed his palms together like sandpaper on wood. "I'll help you. I have the connections, Dustin. But you can't meet the right kind of people in jeans and a T-shirt."

Dustin shook his head and grunted in disdain. "Relationships that mean something? Mean what, exactly? More money? More prestige? A nicer car? I'm never going to be like you, Addison. That's not what I want out of life."

"Perhaps not," Addison agreed with a curt nod. "You and I have traveled different roads. Nevertheless, I do think Ms. Buckley can help you with this trust-fund issue, and I insist you meet with her."

Dustin balked inside, but he didn't let it show. He didn't like being ordered around, especially by members of his family. "How long?"

"Six weeks. That shouldn't be too much of a strain, even for you." Addison began to pace, a sure sign he was losing his patience. Dustin knew his brother didn't like this any better than he did.

And why should he? Dustin knew Addison wasn't a bully at heart, childhood pranks notwithstanding. He was as pinched by their father's will as anyone.

Better to wrap things up and let Addison

get on his way. Back to work in his posh office, where he was more in his element.

"At the end of the six weeks, then, I get my inheritance money?"

Addison met his gaze straight on, staring as if trying to read his soul. Dustin let him look, knowing his own expression was unreadable. It was something he'd practiced.

"You know I'm taking a calculated risk here." Addison cleared his throat and continued pacing back and forth in front of Dustin, his arms clasped behind his back. "And I expect a full return on my investment."

"Meaning?"

"I want you to cooperate with Ms. Buckley fully. If she gives me a bad report, I will put your trust fund on hold and you won't be able to touch it."

Dustin opened his mouth to protest against these rules, but Addison held one hand up, palm out. He clearly didn't want to be interrupted.

"If, however, you make a genuine effort toward your reform, the money is yours, with no limitations from me or anyone. I know that's what you want. You just have to make an effort."

He gave Dustin a genuine smile, but

Dustin just winced at his brother's stilted effort.

"This will work, Dustin, if you just give it half a chance."

Dustin clenched his jaw tightly, still hardly believing his brother had set up such a scheme. Addison wasn't married — he was as careful in dating as Dustin himself was. And for good reason.

Every woman in the world wanted to change a man; it was in their very nature to meddle that way. Every man alive knew that, and ran from it with his whole being until he inevitably got caught in some woman's snare.

It was the extraordinary, seesaw-like balance between men and women that Dustin didn't even try to comprehend, and generally attempted to steer away from.

That was at least partly the reason Dustin remained single at age thirty. His experience with relationships with the opposite sex had, frankly, made him more than a little world-wise when it came to women.

He liked being on his own, being his own man and answerable to no one but himself and God.

And for some strange woman to get paid for meddling in his private affairs, pushing her ideals on him — what kind of woman would take such a job?

This Isobel Buckley must be on a real power trip. He could only guess at what kinds of torture she would concoct for him.

Still, it was only six weeks.

What could happen in six weeks?

CHAPTER THREE

Isobel was more than a little anxious about meeting the man she'd heard so much about. With all she'd been told, she had absolutely no idea what to expect when she actually met the real person.

Dustin Fairfax.

She had thoughtfully recommended a public venue for their first meeting, knowing both of them would feel a bit more comfortable with other people around, especially at this first encounter.

She admitted being nervous herself, at least inwardly, which was silly, really. She did this for a living, after all.

But this was different. The nuances weren't lost on her, and she was certain they weren't lost on *him,* either. Dustin wasn't coming to her for her expertise and help — or at least it was not his idea to do so — and she wasn't even certain he was coming willingly.

Camille and Addison had made the arrangements, and here she sat, in a quiet deli on 16th Street, waiting for Dustin to show up.

If he actually materialized.

She still wasn't convinced he was a willing guinea pig in this experiment, and that fact was something she meant to establish before this day was over. She wouldn't blame him if he found somewhere else to be and didn't make their meeting at all.

He was already twelve minutes late to their appointment, not that she was counting. She tried to distract herself by watching the people around her, the usual eclectic hodgepodge of faces and accents that made Denver so interesting. Coffee shops were the best for finding interesting people to view.

But no matter how hard she tried, her gaze kept straying back to the front door, her adrenaline rushing every time the bell indicated a new customer was entering or exiting.

She had purposefully taken a seat at a corner table where she could easily see the entrance. She wanted to have a moment to watch Dustin before they were formally introduced.

She wiped her palms against her conservative navy blue, calf-length-split rayon skirt, ostensibly to straighten it — for at least the tenth time. She straightened her back and adjusted her posture, an incidental habit she was hardly aware of but often performed.

Suddenly a man burst through the door like a Tasmanian devil, lifting his hat and scrubbing his hands through his thick black hair. He looked around, his eyes sweeping across the tables with a glazed, harried look.

He was obviously searching for someone, and he definitely fit the profile she'd been given for Mr. Fairfax — six feet tall, medium build, black hair, green eyes.

Isobel froze, not giving any indication she saw him at all. She lowered her eyes to the table and pinched her lips.

She was afraid this was how it would be.

Her first impression wasn't good.

Dustin's black hair, what she could see of it from under a backward-faced, navy newsboy cap, was long — nearly shoulder length — and thick and curly. She wondered if anyone had ever told him his hairstyle had gone out in the eighties.

Way out.

The thought made her laugh, and she politely covered her mouth with her hand.

His big green eyes were friendly, though,

and he was smiling. Those were immediate pluses, in her book. Not many people faced life with a grin these days. It was a rare blessing to see.

Polishing up the outside of a man would be a piece of cake for her, but how could she ever hope to turn some weirdo into a socialite?

Apparently, that was one worry she could cross off her list. Kindness showed in every line of his face. Somehow, after seeing him in person, she felt in her heart she could work with him.

His clothes were another matter.

He was attired in faded, holey blue jeans and a navy blue T-shirt that had seen better days. She couldn't even decipher the writing on the front. And his old tennis shoes — once white, as far as she could guess, but now a scuffed gray — were abominable.

She bit her bottom lip thoughtfully. Part of her screamed to duck under the table, however ungracefully, and hide from the man. Back out of the plan. Get away from it all.

But then she remembered her purpose here, and with this thought came resolution. This was a job like any other job, however different in form it — *he* — presented itself.

It was time to buck up and do what she was hired to do.

Of course, Dustin was an unconventional scalawag who was continually late to his appointments. Hadn't she discussed this very thing with Addison and Camille? Why else would Addison feel compelled to hire an image consultant to clean him up and generally organize his life for him?

And how hard could it be, really?

Her mind was already envisioning a sharp pair of scissors in her hand, lopping off great handfuls of his thick black hair. Her smile widened.

"Mr. Fairfax," she called, waving her hand. "Over here."

The man turned at her voice and smiled as he approached. "Please, call me Dustin," he said, his voice deep and resonant. "All my friends do. And you must be *Iz-a-belle,*" he said, pronouncing her name with a crisp Italian accent. His emphasis was strongly on the last syllable. "Belle. It has a nice ring to it." He laughed at his own joke, but Isobel just shook her head.

She stared at him for a moment, trying to get her bearings. No one had ever, in the whole course of her life, called her Belle before.

Everyone, even her mother, called her Isobel. Camille called her Izzy sometimes, but they had known each other forever.

"Isobel Buckley," she corrected subtly, hoping he'd take the hint.

"Dustin Fairfax," he said, turning his chair around and straddling it. "But of course, you already know my name."

"Yes," she agreed mildly, linking her fingers on the tabletop to keep from fidgeting. It was important that Dustin have confidence in her dignity and refinement if he was going to take any advice from her. It wasn't his problem she was feeling as if she were walking on shaky ground at the moment.

"Don't feel awkward on my account," he said with a wink.

Despite herself, her heart fluttered. The man was certainly a charmer, if a badly dressed one. And how had he known she was feeling off-kilter? Had he seen it in her expression? She determined then and there to take better control of herself and the situation.

She cleared her throat and looped a lock of her deep brown hair around her index finger, twirling it in lazy circles. "Let's start at the beginning," she suggested.

"Sounds reasonable," he agreed. That he was genuinely amicable was clearly apparent to Isobel and worked immediately in his favor. He appeared unusually relaxed and free of the usual stark brassiness most men his age wore about themselves like a cloak.

Dustin was simply himself, and he offered that openness willingly to her; and, she suspected, to all those he encountered in the — what was it?

Oh, yes. *Flower shop.*

If she was successful in her endeavor, she very well could be about to change all that. It was one of the things his brother had mentioned — in the negative category of Dustin's life.

One small shop was all he owned. He didn't even have a second one located across town at one of the many available malls and outlets.

She felt a shiver she couldn't identify as anticipation or warning.

"You were late," she said without preamble. She had to start somewhere.

"I had the worst time finding a place to park," he explained with a shrug and an easy grin. "You know how Denver parking can be."

"You drove your *car?*" Isobel asked, surprise seeping into her voice.

"Doesn't everybody?"

She knew he was teasing her, but she

couldn't resist answering him. "I assumed — well — that you could walk here from your shop. Or take the mall bus, although I admit that doesn't appeal to me, either."

His grin widened. "I did walk. My shop is only a few blocks down from here. But what would have been the fun in telling you that?" He chuckled. "I drove my car to work, though, since I live in the suburbs. I'm telling you this in case you want to tool around in it later." He gave her a wide, cheesy grin.

Dustin was clearly on the far side of sense. What had she gotten herself into?

"As I'm sure you'll quickly learn," he clarified, "I'm not everybody. Run-of-the-mill does not apply to me. I often walk, but I have a nifty little sports car and I like to drive it."

"Oh," she said lamely.

"And you came in . . . ?"

The question dangled before her, taunting her silently for an answer.

She blushed. "A Towncar."

"Yeah? Huh. Well, what do you know? That doesn't surprise me in the least. You look the type. You wouldn't catch me dead in a Towncar, though."

"Why is that?" she asked, intrigued despite wondering if his attitude might be condescending to her. It didn't show in his tone or facial expression. His smile was genuine and kind. He had a strong, masculine smile that made her heart beat faster in response.

He was pulling her under his spell and she knew it, but she was helpless to stop herself. Maybe that was exactly what he wanted, and she was playing right into his hand, but she'd never been as cynical as she oftentimes thought she should be.

She immediately decided to take Dustin at face value unless he proved her wrong. It was only fair, and he seemed nice enough.

She cupped her chin in one palm and leaned forward to better hear his answer.

"Well, I can't afford it, for one thing," he said. "At least, not until I get my inheritance." He laughed at his own joke. "And for another, I think fancy cars give off kind of a hoity-toity attitude to the general public, don't you?"

Isobel nearly choked. Towncars were a regular, accepted part of her existence as an image consultant, and something she'd taken for granted. She had been raised in a small Texas town and had not grown up with such luxuries, yet she admitted now she'd never given a single thought to how a person on the streets of Denver, perhaps someone less fortunate than herself, would consider the mode of transportation she chose.

"But you said you drive a sports car," she countered tightly as it occurred to her. It was an accusation, and she knew it sounded like one.

"That's true. I do," he said, smiling. He didn't look the least bit offended, but he offered no further explanation.

"And that's okay with you."

His grin widened. Then he lifted his dark eyebrows and shrugged.

"Are you hungry?" Dustin asked, meeting her gaze squarely. She had the feeling he knew exactly what she was thinking and was playing rescuer to her own guilty conscience.

It was an unnerving feeling. She shook her mind from the thought and said, "No, thank you. I try not to eat much after noon."

He glanced at his watch, as if he weren't already aware it was well after the noon hour. "You're kidding. That can't be good for your health."

Isobel chuckled. Ten minutes into their first conversation and *he* was already trying to change *her.* What an amusing paradox.

"A drink, at least?" he coaxed in a warm, rich voice. "You aren't going to sit across from me with nothing while I stuff my face, are you? I missed lunch and I'm starving."

"All right," she said, giving in gracefully to this one small concession. "I guess I might enjoy a good cup of hot tea. Herbal. And make sure it has no caffeine or sugar."

He stood and saluted. "Yes, ma'am. I'll bring you just what you ordered."

"Thank you, Dustin," she said with a sigh as she watched him approach the counter. She wasn't sure if he'd heard her or not, for he didn't turn or acknowledge the comment.

"Dearest Lord, what have I gotten myself into?" she prayed under her breath as she stared at Dustin's broad back. "I'm feeling a little overwhelmed here. This is a new one for me. A little help? Please."

Actually, she could use a *lot* of help. She felt she was way out of her league where Dustin Fairfax was concerned.

He quickly returned to the table with a loaded tray, placing it on the table before turning his chair around properly and seating himself.

"One cool-mint hot tea for you, and two large, completely indigestible pastrami sandwiches with extra jalapenos and onions, extra-large French fries and a large cola for me."

With a cheeky smile he leaned on his

elbows and began unwrapping his first sandwich.

"Are you *trying* to give yourself a heart attack?" she quipped.

He burst into laughter and had to cover his mouth to keep from spitting food. Putting his index finger in the air in a gesture for her to hold on for a moment, he chewed and swallowed his large bite of sandwich, then chased it down with a big drink of cola.

"This stuff doesn't bother me," he assured her. "I'm as healthy as a horse."

She eyed his meal in disbelief, then twisted her lips and met his sparkling gaze. "Right. Tell me those same words again in ten years."

"I had my cholesterol checked when I turned thirty. Honest."

She shrugged. "Eat whatever you want. They're your arteries."

With a grin, he picked up his jumbo-sized sandwich and took another big bite, right out of the middle of the bread.

Etiquette was evidently going to have to be added to Isobel's list of things to go over with Dustin in their six weeks together.

She was amazed at how fast the sandwiches and fries disappeared, especially since Dustin was doing most of the talking during the meal.

He cheerfully talked about his childhood — about growing up in the Fairfax household, how he had felt having a controlling father and a competitive older brother like Addison around.

He glossed over the death of his mother, though Isobel thought it must have made a huge alteration in the life of a considerate, impressionable young man, both then and now. Certainly such a tragic event would have had a great deal of influence on the man Dustin had become.

Addison was Dustin's only sibling, and according to Dustin's many laughter-filled stories, they had done their share of fighting and wrestling when they were young. Addison had always been bigger, but Dustin was slick, smooth and, he told Isobel with a smile that could spark up a lighthouse, he could run faster. So the disputes had remained fairly even, and Dustin spoke of his brother with affection.

He asked Isobel about her family, but she said as little as possible, other than that she was an only child and grew up in a small town in Texas.

Since Dustin's parents had been together forty-five years until his mother's death, Isobel felt awkward discussing her own parents' divorce when she was an infant, and the many ways that had affected her.

Besides, everyone's parents got divorced these days. Why should she have been any different?

She didn't remember her father, and though she'd made peace with that, it rose up to haunt her now. She felt overly emotional trying to discuss her childhood, though Dustin had been open about his.

Not that she'd had a bad life — her mother had become a Christian soon after her father had left, and Isobel had been raised healthy, happy and loved, with plenty of hard work to bind them together in strength and lots of support from their home church.

Still, she didn't like talking about it, especially to a man she hardly knew. She didn't even want to think about it.

When she said as much, Dustin seemed to take it in stride, though he tried time and again to engage her in talking about herself; if not her childhood, at least what she was doing now.

"I have a small condo in the city that I share with my best friend, Camille. Have you met her?" she asked inquisitively.

He shook his head vigorously. "No, but I've heard she's a great girl."

"Camille would have a fit if she heard you

calling her *girl,*" Isobel replied. "We're both twenty-eight, you know."

"Oh," he said, frowning as he strung out the syllable. "*Old* ladies, then."

She couldn't help it. She kicked him under the table, and thought she made good contact with his shin.

He didn't even acknowledge that he'd been kicked at all, except perhaps in the tiniest widening of his all-male grin.

"I have the rest of the afternoon off," he said with his usual casual bluntness. "If you want to take advantage of me, that is."

Isobel choked on her tea. She knew her face was flaming, and it didn't help that Dustin only chuckled mildly when he realized what he'd said, or rather, how it had sounded.

He shook his head and cuffed the side of his head to indicate he hadn't been thinking. "What I was really trying to say was —"

"I know what you were trying to say," she said, surprised she could speak. "And I'm going to surprise you by taking you up on that invitation, however awkwardly it may have been worded," she teased, enjoying the way his attractive smile widened when their eyes met.

She fought a grin as she considered her

plan. Oh, she would take advantage of Dustin, all right — or rather, of his easygoing nature.

Isobel was certain she could make him a changed man in a single afternoon. She thought even Addison would be impressed, not to mention pleased, with such a feat.

Maybe Dustin would get his inheritance after all, if she had anything to do with it.

And she did.

CHAPTER FOUR

"Do you want to take a ride in my sports car?" Dustin offered, jingling the keys in his pocket as he held the deli door open for her and gestured her through ahead of him.

She glanced up at the dim sunlight. At least it didn't look as if it was going to rain, or worse, snow. Colorado winters were unpredictable. "Tempting as the offer sounds, a ride won't be necessary. We can walk where we're going."

As soon as they stepped out onto the sidewalk, he automatically repositioned himself so he was walking closer to the curb. The sign of a true gentleman, Isobel thought. Maybe this wouldn't be so hard after all.

Dustin kept his hands in his pockets and whistled as he walked, glancing at her from time to time and genuinely smiling, although a bit as if he had a secret he wasn't yet ready to share with her. He seemed in no hurry, but rather content just to walk slowly and casually, as if they were old friends.

And he was certainly taking this well, having to make sudden changes in his life dictated by another person he had only just met and had no reason yet to trust.

If she were in his position, she knew she would be balking and pulling at the reins at such outrageous and uncomfortable demands.

Then again, maybe he didn't really know what he was getting himself into.

Yet.

She stopped and gestured at a shop door. "We're here."

Dustin glanced up at the sign and froze.

"No way," he said, his voice low and guttural. "No possible way."

"Now, Dustin, be reasonable," she pleaded, reaching up to place a hand on his shoulder, hoping he would take the hint and look at her.

He did.

And when their eyes met, Isobel felt exactly what he was feeling — the shock, the panic, the desire to run.

Truth told, she felt like running, herself, and pulling him along. But that wasn't what she was here to do, and Dustin had to start somewhere. Here was as good a spot as any.

She would not back down, no matter how his bright green puppy-dog eyes implored her to do so.

"It's not as bad as all that," she assured him, not certain how committed she sounded.

He shook his head. "Says you."

"Trust me?" she urged.

His gaze asked, *Why should I?* His jaw was clenched, but he stepped forward and opened the door for her. "After you."

She grinned in triumph, her heart pumping at the battle of wills she had just fought and won. This was a big victory for her — her first — and would no doubt be one of her best. It would pave the way for other small successes and triumphs.

The end result, of course, would be a final product of which she could be proud — and more importantly, of which *Dustin* could be proud.

"Ricardo, please meet my friend, Dustin," Isobel said as her regular hairdresser rushed forward and kissed both her hands.

Ricardo was unique and not a little odd with his spiked purple hair and dozens of gold necklaces that encompassed his broad, hairy chest, not to mention his bombastic personality and shrill voice.

His personality and flashy looks took some getting used to, but when it came to hair, Ricardo was the best in the industry.

Dustin, his eyebrows raised and his expression one of pure panic, was halfway out the door before Isobel caught him by the elbow.

"No way," he whispered in her ear. "Look at that guy's hair. I'm not letting him anywhere near me with a pair of scissors. He obviously has no clue what he's doing."

She laughed. "Hairdressers don't do their own hair," she said, nudging him back into the room. "Haven't you ever heard the elementary-school logic problem about the small town with only two barbers?"

He looked at her as if she'd gone mad. She smothered a smile.

"Obviously not." She burst into laughter at the horrified, stubborn look on his face. He was adorable when he was being mulish.

With a flourish of her arms, she continued with her story. "So, then. There were only two barbers in this small town. One of the barbers had a neat trim, and the other's hair was chopped at odd edges. Now think about it, Dustin. Which of these two barbers would you rather go to?"

Delighted, she was aware of how his eyes

immediately began to sparkle with understanding and his amused gaze turned on her.

He chuckled and shook his head. "I've never heard that one before, and I'll admit you have a valid point. But then again, I have no reason to trust Ricardo, despite your clever stories." He winked at her. "I haven't seen the other barber, so to speak," he reminded her, his voice grave but his eyes alight with humor.

"Oh, yes, you have," she countered, grinning back at him. She ran her fingers through the thick lengths of her long, chocolate-brown hair, circling the ends with her fingers. "You're looking at her."

"*That* man does your hair?" he said in an incredulous whisper. "Surely not."

"Oh, but he does. Ricardo is a genius. He not only cuts my hair, but he has a clientele list that would blow your mind. The best haircuts in Denver are provided by this man, I assure you."

Dustin yanked off his newsboy cap and scratched the top of his head, still looking as if he might bolt. "I can't believe I'm doing this," he muttered.

Isobel wordlessly took his arm and led him farther into the hair studio. Ricardo, who had no doubt heard most of their conversation, elegantly gestured to a barber chair and indicated Dustin should sit. Isobel was surprised the hairstylist's expression didn't betray a thing.

He drew a smock around Dustin and directed his gaze to Isobel. "What would you like done with the young man, my dear?"

"His hair," Isobel joked.

"Really?" Ricardo made a gesture of surprise, his hands over his mouth. "And here I was all ready to give him a pedicure."

Dustin's eyes widened and his jaw dropped at what he no doubt considered a threat. Pinching his mouth closed with a frustrated twist to his lips, he quickly tucked his feet under the smock, making Ricardo howl with unabashed laughter.

"Cut it short," said Isobel decisively, and Dustin cringed, shirking his shoulders and glaring first at her and then at Ricardo.

She paused a minute to let him stew before continuing her direction to Ricardo, not allowing herself the satisfied smile she was feeling inside.

"Not too short, though. A business cut. Something to keep his curls in order. And he's still young — keep the front long enough to comb back."

"I'm going to look like a toddler," Dustin

grumbled good-naturedly.

"Not with Ricardo's help, you won't," she assured him, moving forward to place a hand on his shoulder. "He is perfection itself."

She turned halfway away from him and muttered, "Not like you *could* look like a toddler."

"What was that?" Dustin asked immediately, sounding suspicious.

She turned back to him and grinned. "Oh, nothing. I was just thinking aloud."

Dustin's gaze met hers in the large mirror in front of them. He still didn't look convinced.

"Trust me," she pleaded. "I really do know what I'm doing."

He gave her a clipped nod.

Knowing no amount of verbal persuasion would help, she stepped back then and let the master hairdresser go to his work.

The first thing Ricardo did, after giving Dustin a thorough shampoo and returning him to his chair, was to turn Dustin away from the mirror, which Isobel immediately understood and thought was an excellent idea. The worst thing that could happen would be for Dustin to run out before his haircut was finished.

Half a haircut would definitely not be an

improvement on no haircut at all. She curled her fingers around in front of her mouth to hide her amusement, but Dustin caught her motion and glared at her anyway.

Dustin closed his eyes as Ricardo trimmed the back of his hair flush with his neckline. The more the hairdresser snipped, the curlier Dustin's hair became, but they were soft, natural curls instead of the long, frizzier style he'd worn before.

Finally, Ricardo dropped a bottle of hair gel into Dustin's lap without a word.

"What am I supposed to do with this?" Dustin growled, picking up the bottle and eyeing it suspiciously. "I'm a wash-and-wear kind of guy."

"Allow me to demonstrate," Ricardo said, not taking no for an answer. "You put a nickel-sized amount of the product on your palm and then work it through the tips of your hair with your fingers. Work the hair up and out. There is no need to work it into your scalp."

The hairdresser took the bottle from Dustin and held out his palm. He squirted a dollop of orange gel in the exact shape and size of a nickel, dropped the bottle back in Dustin's lap, then rubbed his hands together and began stroking his fingers expertly through Dustin's hair.

Dustin was still staring at his lap, hardly watching what Ricardo was doing. "I've never in my life . . ." he said, sounding stunned, or at least stubbornly uncomfortable.

"There's a first time for everything, right, Dustin?" Isobel asked quietly, totally amazed at his transformation. "Take a look at yourself."

Holding her breath for his response, Isobel turned Dustin's chair back toward the mirror.

Dustin stared at his reflection, hardly recognizing the man staring back at him. Who was this slick-haired man?

Perhaps he *had* worn his hair in the same style for a few years longer than he should have. Isobel may have had a point.

Of course, that was her job, wasn't it? To find the best places to make changes in order to make him a better man?

He still wasn't completely sold on the idea, but this was one point in her favor.

That said, he wasn't at all convinced about putting sticky orange gel in his hair every morning. But he had to admit the guy staring back at him in the mirror had his own charm.

Between the haircut and the gel Ricardo had meticulously applied, the hairdresser had done an outstanding job taming the wild curls Dustin had battled all his life. Ricardo had parted his hair just off to the right side of center and combed every strand of hair neatly back into place. Only a few stray curls escaped.

As Isobel had instructed, the hair on his forehead was combed back in the current style. He had to admit it looked good, though he wasn't at all sure he could duplicate the process when he was alone in his own home.

But in the end, the score was: Isobel one, and Dustin zero.

He stared in the mirror one more second, memorizing every detail.

He looked, well, contemporary.

And though there was no way he would admit it to anyone — especially Isobel, who would no doubt report such findings straight to Addison — Dustin found he rather liked his new look.

Especially with a hat.

"Double or nothing," he mumbled under his breath with a quick shake of his head.

"What was that?" she queried back, looking wary and more than a little suspicious.

He adjusted his newsboy cap backward on top of his new haircut, winked at Isobel and walked out the door without a word.

CHAPTER FIVE

Dustin didn't wait for Isobel to call him. Part of him — probably the sensible part — wanted to hide from her and tenaciously avoid her for as much of the prescribed six weeks as possible, but something about Isobel intrigued him. Completely apart from the stupid agreement he'd made with Addison, perhaps even in spite of it, he wanted to get to know her better.

Besides, in the long run it *was* the only way to get to his trust fund. He wouldn't examine his motives any deeper than that.

Isobel was certainly a beautiful woman, with her deep brown hair filled with red highlights and her warm brown eyes. She was tall and lithe. Maybe she could stand to gain a pound or two, in his opinion, but she still had the hint of womanly curves that would turn any man's head.

What caught him most, though, were her gorgeous bee-stung lips and knockout smile, especially when it was directed at him.

Perhaps it was this thought that made him hold his breath as he dialed her number.

"Dustin," she said when he greeted her. She sounded surprised, but did he hear a bit of excitement in her voice, as well, or was it his imagination and a healthy dose of wishful thinking? "I certainly didn't expect to hear from you so s-soon," she stammered.

"Well, I figured you owe me one." He waited for her response, a grin pulling at his lips.

Dead silence.

He listened to the telephone line crackling and the praise music in the background, obviously coming from Isobel's stereo.

"Look at it this way. I put up with your torture yesterday, so today you're on my terms. And that's why I'm calling." He chuckled.

"That's not how this scheme is supposed to work," she protested immediately in a high, strained voice that only made Dustin's smile widen. "We're not supposed to be having a social relationship. I'm working on you, remember?"

"How are you going to help me become an honest, hard-working citizen if you don't know anything about me?" he countered.

"Granted, you chopped off my hair without even knowing my middle name, but I don't think you can turn me into the best I can become without knowing a little bit more about the *real* me."

"What *is* your middle name?" she asked, sounding distinctly uncomfortable.

"So, you want to know now, do you? *After* you whack my hair off?" he teased. "How fair is that?"

"Dustin," she pleaded.

"James."

"Dustin James Fairfax. That's very nice. Now I will know that crucial bit of information for future whacking and/or cutting."

"Is that a threat?"

"Oh, no," she said with a laugh. "Consider it a promise."

"That doesn't sound good," he said. "Even more reason for us to get together today, though, if you ask me. Which you didn't," he pointed out wryly.

She sighed extravagantly. Pointedly.

"What did you have in mind?" She sounded as if he were about to ask her to walk the plank.

The horrible pirate captain. That was him, all right. Fit him like an old pair of sneakers. He held in the callous chuckle that

70

would befit his pirate status, but he was tempted.

Instead, he told her why he'd really called. "I thought you could join me at my flower shop. To see what I do all day, you know? The regular nine-to-five thing my brother doesn't really think I have going on."

She breathed an audible sigh of relief, and this time it sounded genuine. "That actually sounds reasonable."

"And you sound surprised."

She laughed. "Perhaps I shouldn't be. I have an active imagination. You'll learn that about me as we work together. I'm more tempted to believe the moon is made of green cheese than that astronauts have landed."

"I thought so — something like me holding you at sword point as you walk the plank?"

"Mmm. Something like that," she murmured thoughtfully.

"Aaargh," he said playfully in his best gravelly pirate's voice.

Dustin gave her directions to his shop on the 16th Street Mall, and they planned to meet at ten o'clock, a half hour away.

In the meantime, Dustin set out to fix his hair, which he had been ignoring until this point, since no one had been going to see him. At least no one who would care.

His old style had been easy — shower, comb it and leave it alone. But this hairstyling business — this was new to him.

And yet he had to make the effort. For the acquisition of his trust fund. He would do well to remember his true purpose in this six-week make-a-new-man-out-of-him process — getting his money.

Why then, as he combed through his hair, did he think his primping and preening might have just a little to do with Isobel, the woman?

He used the gel, but that only made his hair worse.

Every single hair on his head was sticking up, and from Dustin's viewpoint, each and every strand was going in a different direction from all the others.

He looked like a startled porcupine.

Dustin was befuddled. Ricardo had made it look so easy.

With a frustrated growl, he picked up the gel bottle and squirted another large dollop of gel into his palm, then slathered it through his hair.

Now his hair was not only prickly, but stiff as a needle. He took his bristle brush, the one he'd used for years, and slicked his hair back.

Oh, boy.

He gave his reflection a sinister look with shaded eyes and a whacky half smile.

This was better, if he were going for the crazy-man look.

He sighed aloud and began to part his hair on the side. Curls immediately began popping up, but he thought he looked better than he had before, if only marginally.

Less than a half hour later, Dustin was in the back room of his shop, designing a floral arrangement for an upcoming wedding, when Isobel showed up, making her way slowly through his shop and appearing to take in everything. She stopped several times to admire one bouquet or another, even leaning forward to inhale the fragrance of the sweet-smelling blooms.

When she reached his work table in the back of the shop, she stood silently, watching him as he selected various flowers and placed them in an eye-catching manner within the arrangement.

"You're very talented," she said softly, stepping forward.

"Thanks," he responded, grinning at her. "It's a great way to express my creativity. Arranging flowers is something I particularly enjoy."

"I would hope so, considering you own

this place," she teased. "If you hated flowers, I would have a real problem trying to reform you, now wouldn't I?"

"I meant it's one of many things that bring joy to my life," he corrected with a laugh.

"Oh," she said softly. Then, obviously trying to change the subject, she gestured at the vase he was working on. "That looks complicated."

"It's not just putting flowers together," he explained, handing her five yellow carnations and gesturing to the arrangement. "It's so much more. If you let it be, flower arranging can be a real work of art, like painting or sculpting."

Isobel clutched the flower stems, wondering what he meant for her to do with them. She'd come here today, as he had put it, to see him in his natural environment, so to speak, and to assess what needed to be done in the remaining six weeks.

She'd certainly not come to arrange flowers, and she had not the least idea what she was doing. Her artistic tendencies, such as they were, leaned toward fashion, not flora.

She eyed Dustin, who merely gestured toward the arrangement and grinned. "It's for a wedding," he informed her, adjusting a bloom here and there as he spoke. "The bridesmaids will be in yellow."

"Hence the yellow carnations," she said, winking back at him. "But please don't expect me to place these flowers in the arrangement. I'm sure I'll do it wrong, and then you'll just have to start it all over again."

"How will you know unless you try?" he asked quietly, but with emphasis. "Give it a go, Belle. It will tell me a lot about you."

He gestured at the unfinished bouquet. "The worst that can happen is that I'll have to help you, and I really don't mind doing that. It's a risk I'm willing to take," he said with a chuckle.

She flashed him a surprised look at the nickname, but didn't comment on it.

Dustin was trying to figure *her* out. Why would he do that? Everything felt all backward, and Isobel's stomach was filled with psychopathic butterflies.

She was supposed to be analyzing *him.*

It suddenly occurred to her that perhaps an attempt at working a flower bouquet would do just that. Give her a chance to see him interact with her as she destroyed his beautiful floral arrangement with her incompetence.

Would he become angry, or was he more of a patient man? Isobel would bet on the latter, but there was no time like the present to see for sure.

She stepped forward and tentatively began placing carnations carefully within the arrangement, gently and one at a time.

Dustin whistled low and clapped his hands slowly and in rhythm, each touch of his palms echoing in the large, colorful room and reverberating through Isobel's heart. "I knew it."

She looked up from her work, surprised, and met his gaze. "Knew what?" she asked, her mind half-distracted with her work.

"That you're a natural artist."

"You're kidding," she said honestly, feeling somehow elevated by his heartfelt praise. "I've never done this before. The closest I've come to flower arranging has been jamming a bouquet of flowers I bought at the grocery store into a vase."

Dustin laughed and then winked at her as the bell rang over the door, indicating customers were entering the store.

Isobel stood quietly by as Dustin assisted several of his obviously well-appreciated clientele, some of whom looked to be affluent, and many of whom had just walked in off the street amidst their 16th Street shopping.

This was what Isobel had been waiting for. It was an excellent opportunity to observe Dustin in his natural surroundings, when he was dealing with his everyday life and not her chaotic uprooting of his life, and she took advantage of the moment.

Oddly enough, she found herself enjoying her perusal of the man in his natural environment.

The first thing she noticed about Dustin was that his smile never left his face. Nothing seemed to ruffle him — not an irate customer being, in Isobel's opinion, absolutely ridiculous in her demands and refusing to calm down despite his best efforts. Not even this forced intrusion of Isobel into his life disrupted his careful attitude as she attempted to turn a frog into a prince.

Part of her problem, she thought — glad she was watching him from a distance and he would not be able to see her expression — was that Dustin was one very cute frog.

Even in faded blue jeans and a plain black T-shirt, Dustin was a man that women would naturally notice — *and* find attractive.

He wasn't handsome, at least not in the classic sense of the word, but something about him drew Isobel to him, and she knew she couldn't possibly be the only woman who felt that way.

Dustin was irresistible in the way of a

tough, self-reliant stray tomcat. Not necessarily in the mood for a cuddle, but ready to jump in and stir things up.

And though he was big and independent, his green eyes emanated warmth and kindness, and that attracted Isobel more than any of his physical features could.

And then there was his hair.

She thought he looked infinitely more approachable with this new cut. He had obviously tried to emulate Ricardo in recreating the style, but he'd used too much gel and his hair looked stiff and stubbornly unmovable.

Even so, a few curls slipped out, the most noticeable of which was the curl across his forehead. She had the *most* indescribable urge to brush that lock of hair back where it belonged.

Suddenly, she realized the store was empty and she was still staring at Dustin.

Only, now he was staring back, and his green-eyed gaze was full of amusement.

He approached her slowly. "What do you think?" he asked, standing so close to her she could smell the cinnamon gum he was chewing.

She didn't want Dustin guessing what she was really thinking, so she glazed him with her most cheerful smile and said, "Oh, I don't know."

He lifted an eyebrow, silently challenging her off-the-cuff explanation.

She paused, searching for the right words. "Charming. Absolutely charming."

That she was talking about *him* and not the shop would be left unsaid. She could hardly be expected to think straight when his gleaming eyes so cheerfully held her gaze. She barely remembered to breathe.

He smiled. "Why, thank you, ma'am," he said with a put-on western drawl as he tipped an imaginary cowboy hat to her. "Glad you like it. I'm rather fond of the place myself."

Isobel chuckled. Addison had indicated that Dustin didn't put enough time and effort into his work, but Isobel saw he was wrong.

Dustin cared a great deal.

"The shop looks very successful," she said thoughtfully, hoping her astonishment didn't register on her face or in her voice.

From everything she'd been told about Dustin, she admitted — at least to herself — that she had pegged him for a flighty man who couldn't settle down or make a commitment to anything.

So it was no surprise that she expected his flower shop to be somewhere between thoroughly disorganized and completely run-down.

She wouldn't make that mistake again.

From now on, the only opinions she would form would be from her own factual observations, and not what she had been told secondhand. As it was, she had a lot of backpedaling to do in order to get to a place she could really start with Dustin.

"I'm here seven days a week," he qualified, as if in answer to her unspoken question, "though I don't always work regular hours. In that sense Addison is right, I guess."

She could stand it no longer. His close proximity was getting to her. He was leaning into her space, so close she could smell his gum.

Taking a deep breath, she clenched her hands together at her sides and pinched her fingernails into her palms, but to no avail. Try as she might, she could not stand it a moment longer.

With one trembling hand, she braced herself against his shoulder. Reaching on tiptoe, she ran her fingers back through his sticky-soft hair and put that stubborn lock of hair back into its rightful position.

"There," she said, stepping back and placing her fists on her hips, happily surveying her handiwork. "Much better."

"I can't promise it will stay that way." As soon as he laughed, the willful curl dropped right back down on his forehead.

"I don't believe it!" she exclaimed. "I just don't believe it."

"Told ya so."

He shrugged, grinning at her stunned expression, and then slowly made his way around the store, straightening items and locking up, whistling a song Isobel recognized but couldn't identify as he worked.

Her heart was in her throat, beating an irregular tattoo as she watched him clear the cash register and prepare his daily deposit. Isobel wondered if this would be the end of Dustin's *planned day* together.

Oddly, though it was past her normal working hours, and though Isobel had gathered more than the amount of information Dustin had meant for her to have, she found herself hoping it wasn't.

Of course, she had a lot of work to do with Dustin's transformation. But really, she admitted privately, she just liked spending time in Dustin's company, and she didn't want the day to end for personal reasons.

He cleared his throat, his back to her as he covered up a display of roses with soft, silky netting. "I, uh — that is — I hope you don't have anywhere you need to be just yet."

Isobel let out the breath she hadn't known she'd been holding. "No, I don't have anything special planned tonight. Why?"

He shrugged and looked away from her, though she caught his secretive smile first. "I thought maybe you could go out with me."

There was a brief, brightly flashing moment when her heart caught in her throat at the words *go out with me* before reality set in.

With a start, she reminded herself of the true relationship between the two of them. She was only here because Dustin's brother had ordered it to be so.

Dustin probably hadn't given any thought to what he was saying. He had simply misphrased his question.

She tried to speak but found her mouth too dry to form words. Clearing her throat, she tried again. She could not — would not allow herself to — make a big deal of nothing. "Where?"

Dustin turned and leaned his back against a wall, one foot flush against the surface.

Isobel's gaze was immediately drawn to his face. His smile was the genuine article. His eyes glowed in the half-light of the security lamps.

Again she considered how attractive he was to her, though not in the conventional way.

Cute.

That's what Dustin Fairfax was. It wasn't a new or currently fashionable term, she was sure, but it *was* Dustin. She'd picked up the word from her youth, when boys would walk by and her girlfriends would exclaim, "Oh, he's so cute!"

And that's what Dustin was, not that Isobel was going to share her newfound insight with him. She had no doubt he'd be appalled by her conclusion.

Men wanted to be thought of as handsome and dashing and strong and mysterious.

Definitely not *cute.*

"I just want to take you for a walk," Dustin answered vaguely, startling Isobel from her reverie.

For a moment she couldn't figure out what he was saying, and then she abruptly remembered she had asked him where he planned to take her this evening.

"It's a nice night for a stroll in downtown Denver. Would you like that?"

She nodded, wondering if he could have presented a scenario which she would have refused. She couldn't think of anything at the moment.

He reached around the cash register and picked up a bouquet of red roses he had prepared, and then escorted her out the back door, locking it securely and turning on the security alarm.

She wondered about the flowers. Did he mean to give them as a gift to her?

She was pleased by the thought.

But if he did plan to give her roses, why had he not done so at the shop?

Maybe he had a special hand-delivery to make, and planned to drop the bouquet off during their stroll.

He was being mysterious again, with that half grin hovering on his face. What was he up to this time?

She wasn't sure she wanted to know.

And yet she did.

"How did you come to be in Denver?" he asked as they walked along the crowded sidewalk. "I know you said you grew up in a small town in Texas. What made you move to a big city?"

"Fashion," she said thoughtfully, but said no more than that.

He chuckled. "Care to elaborate? I'm picturing you following this trail of translucent pink-scarf material until you reached your destination."

"Hmm?" she asked, glancing at him. "Oh, right. Texas." She cringed inside, but quickly determined to give him the short, happy version of her childhood, and leave it at that.

"As I mentioned before, my best friend, Camille, and I grew up in a rural Texas town. I remember summers riding horses from sunup until sunset."

"You learned fashion from riding horses?" he teased lightly.

"No. My mother didn't — Well, my father wasn't around, and so Mom had to work extra hours to keep us afloat. I had a lot of time alone, so I taught myself to sew on my own when I was eight."

"What, uh —" He hesitated. "What happened to your father, if you don't mind my asking?"

She did. But his voice was lined with such sympathy and compassion she knew what he was thinking.

That her father had died.

She should just leave him believing what he liked. She hadn't told any lies.

Exactly.

And if it were anyone else she'd known for less than a week, in any other circumstances but these, she *would* have left well enough alone.

Instead, she found herself blurting out the truth. The whole truth, for once.

"My father left my mother for another woman when I was three years old. They're divorced."

Dustin's tone didn't change. Neither did his expression. "I'm sorry to hear that. Are you close to your father?"

Isobel bit back the retort that sprung to her lips. "I never saw him or heard from him again. Even the government couldn't find him to get him to pay child support."

"I'm sorry," he said simply, and then wrapped her in a warm, tender hug.

Isobel took refuge for a moment in the sheer masculine strength of his embrace. Slowly the bitterness eating at her heart began to crumble.

Dustin was so strong, like a fortress against her painful thoughts. She felt safe in his arms.

But she wouldn't cry. Not for her father. She'd decided that long ago.

He wasn't worth it.

At length she straightened her shoulders and broke the embrace. Dustin immediately stepped back, his face awash with pity and compassion.

Isobel did not want to be pitied, not even by Dustin.

Especially not by Dustin.

But his next words put her back at ease. "So, you said you taught yourself to sew. You must really have a gift for it — from God. I'd love it if you would tell me more about it."

It took her a moment to compose herself.

"Mom had a sewing machine she'd kept packed up away in the attic. One day Camille and I decided to be explorers. High adventurers, you know?"

Dustin chuckled.

"So, we visited the attic and found the sewing machine. I was instantly in love. I instinctively knew how to use it. I can't explain it to you, except perhaps that it was trial and error. And I did instinctively know a lot of things, as if it were already placed in my mind for me to use."

Dustin grinned. "God," he said firmly.

"God," she agreed. "Anyway, the work kept me busy. And happy. I always had a knack for knowing what was in fashion. As you said more than once, I believe it is, for me, a gift from God. And I thank Him for it every day of my life."

"Amen," Dustin said softly and fervently under his breath, though not so low that Isobel was unable to hear it.

Suddenly he stopped and tugged on her

elbow to get her to stop, as well. "We're here. This will be perfect for what I have in mind."

What he had in mind? What in the world was that supposed to mean?

Isobel looked around her, puzzled. People buzzed in and out of shops and up and down the sidewalks, reminding Isobel of a swarm of bees. None of the shops looked like somewhere Dustin would deliver flowers, but she shrugged. What did she know about the business?

Everyone everywhere had a sweetheart, it seemed. Why not someone in one of these quirky shops?

"All right, so now what?" she queried, flashing him a confused smile. At least he'd gotten her thinking about something other than her father's cruel betrayal.

He grinned back, his eyes gleaming with mystery. "Now," he said, "we go down there."

Isobel's eyes widened as Dustin indicated a long, dark alley she hadn't noticed was there until he pointed to it. It was dark and dank, definitely the sort of place she usually avoided at all costs.

"C'mon, Belle. Bring back some of that adventuresome spirit into your life and let's see the world." Again, he gestured down the alley.

She hung back. The alleyway was so long she couldn't see its end, and the bright light from the streetlamps didn't reach into its darkness.

She was frightened.

She knew she was being ridiculous. She'd taken care of herself all her life. And if that wasn't enough, she had a big, strong man with her. In a real pinch, she trusted Dustin enough to know he would protect her.

But an irrational sense of fear flushed through her nonetheless. Her heart leapt into her throat and lodged there, beating double time.

"No, thank you," she said, her throat tight. "I think I'd rather not accompany you at the moment. I'll just wait out here for you."

Dustin scowled. "Oh, no, you won't, Belle," he said in a low, crackly voice that wouldn't be denied.

And with that, he put his arm around her and gently but firmly, and without giving her the opportunity to protest, led her step by step deeper into the darkness of the bleak, damp alley.

CHAPTER SIX

Dustin gently urged Isobel to follow him around the corner. He kept his grip tight to reassure her and to remind her he was there by her side.

Though she remained silent and walked with her chin high, he sensed he was taking her well out of her comfort zone; although, to be fair, dark alleys were out of *most* people's comfort zones.

Suddenly she clasped a hand on his sleeve, her grip tight. "What are you doing?" she whispered quickly in a low, stiff voice.

"*We* are visiting an old friend," he said with a low chuckle. "Or at least, she'll be a friend once you've met her. Trust me?"

She shrugged and marginally loosened her grip on his sleeve. He knew he had her on that one — it was the same question she'd posed to him just before she'd had all his hair lopped off.

She gave a clipped nod.

Dustin spotted old Rosalinda huddling against an aged brick building, using the side of a large steel trash bin to ward off the nip in the air. The alley was damp, and without the benefit of cleansing sunshine, snow still lingered here and there.

The one wool blanket she apparently owned was wrapped tightly about her shoulders. It was ragged and full of holes. Dustin made a mental note to bring her a new blanket the next time he saw her. Or maybe a sleeping bag.

"Rosalinda," he called, loudly enough for his voice to echo in the alleyway. His intention when he'd yelled was to keep from startling her with his approach, but the old woman jumped to her feet with amazing dexterity for her age and immediately reached for her shopping cart, which Dustin knew contained all her worldly possessions.

For what they were worth.

Not much. Not by anyone's standards. It made his heart ache just to watch her.

He glanced down at Isobel, unsure of her reaction to a situation that was heart-wrenching at best, and wondering not for the first time if he'd made a grave miscalculation in showing her this hidden facet of his life.

He was surprised to see that her eyes were

alight with the emotions he imagined were raging through her as she took in every aspect of the situation.

Fear still glittered in their deep brown depths, but there was another, more prevalent emotion shining through above the fear.

Compassion.

Dustin grinned, his heart pounding as he looked at the beautiful woman at his side. He knew he'd been right about Isobel.

She was as attractive on the inside as she was on the outside.

"It's Dustin." He waved his hand at the old woman and she lifted a hand in response. "I've brought a friend with me."

Isobel raised her hand and waved, offering a quivering smile as she did. She squeezed his hand and stepped close into his shadow. It wasn't, he sensed, that she was afraid of Rosalinda, but rather that she had never been put in this position before.

Perhaps she needed his guidance.

He chuckled and stepped forward. "How are you doing, Rosalinda, sweetheart?" he asked heartily. "You look absolutely stunning."

As he spoke, he plucked a single rose from his bouquet and grinned widely as he presented it to the old woman with a bow and a flourish. "A rose for my Rosalinda."

Isobel hoped her mouth wasn't gaping open. After the initial shock of seeing the poor, tragic state of Rosalinda's circumstances, she had recovered enough to realize Dustin was obviously trying to help in his own adorable, quirky way.

But when he gave her a rose, Isobel's head had gone into a whirl. The gift of a simple flower seemed so completely incongruent with the situation, and yet was such a tender gesture, made so simply and honestly, that it brought tears to her eyes.

And she was not the only one affected by Dustin's gift. Rosalinda's face crinkled into a thousand wrinkles as she flashed her nearly toothless grin.

She reached over and patted Dustin on the back with one gnarled hand. "What would I do without you, Dustin? You always make me smile."

After a moment, Rosalinda turned her attention to Isobel, smiling her gap-toothed smile. "Your young man here never fails to brighten my day."

The first thing to register was that this wasn't Dustin's first visit to the old woman, but rather one of many.

And then the old woman's words hit her with their full impact.

Isobel opened her mouth to speak, to clear

Rosalinda of the grievous misunderstanding that Dustin was *her* young man.

It was odd enough for her to be looked upon as a youngster in the old woman's eyes — she hadn't been called *young* for years — without Rosalinda somehow assuming she had a thing for Dustin.

But just as she was about to clear the air on the inaccuracy, Dustin squeezed her hand and gave an infinitesimal shake of his head.

The message was clear.

Leave it be.

Isobel ruffled as if she were a cat with its hair being brushed the wrong way, but she quickly realized Dustin was probably right.

The old woman almost certainly wouldn't remember the connection between her and Dustin, anyway, though she certainly remembered Dustin from his previous visits to her.

"Here, darling Rosalinda. This'll do you for a spell." Dustin discreetly handed the old woman a folded piece of blue paper.

Rosalinda wrapped one knobby hand around his fist and brought it to her cheek, unabashed at the tears flowing from her eyes.

"Thank you, Dustin," she said with quiet dignity.

"Now, Rosalinda, I've told you before and I'll tell you again, all the thanks belongs to God." He grinned charismatically. "I'll spare you the sermon if you promise to eat. Jesus is the reason, and all that."

"Isn't that a Christmas saying?" Isobel broke in, brushing her hair away from her face with the tips of her fingers. "Jesus is the reason for the season or something like that, right?"

"As far as I'm concerned, it's good all year round," said a laughing Rosalinda. "At least the part he quoted is."

"I second that motion," Dustin added.

"I suppose you're right," Isobel agreed thoughtfully.

Dustin patted Rosalinda on the back and smiled down at her. "Keep the faith."

Isobel could see the faith shining from both her companions, gleaming in their eyes as, one at a time, their gazes met hers.

Every sweet morsel of the scene amazed her — Dustin for having the courage to share his faith in this way and Rosalinda for the courage to recognize her real treasure was in heaven.

Impulsively, she leaned down and patted the woman's hand, an act that was new and foreign to her.

She wasn't the touchy type.

"Thank you," Rosalinda said in her old, crackly voice. She turned her radiant smile upon Isobel.

"But I didn't do anything," Isobel protested, her voice a high, tight squeak. Her heart was pounding a mile a minute.

"Rosalinda, we'll be seeing you again soon," Dustin said, his tone friendly and respectful. "God bless and keep you."

"And you," Rosalinda replied shakily.

Dustin took Isobel's hand and tucked it into the crook of his arm, then turned them both around toward the light of the street.

"You told Rosalinda you didn't do anything for her," he whispered close to her ear. "You're dead wrong about that, you know."

Dustin glanced down at the woman next to him as they stepped into the muted brightness of the streetlamps, stopping her with the touch of his hand as the streamlined mall bus drove past.

Cars weren't allowed on 16th Street, only pedestrian shoppers and the free mall buses, which ran both ways along the street for the convenience of the patrons who didn't wish to walk from end to end of the mall.

Right now, Isobel looked as if she might have run right into that bus if Dustin hadn't stopped her when he did. Her expression gave a brand-new meaning to *dazed and confused.*

He laughed.

She started as if suddenly awakened.

"What's so funny?" she asked warily, pulling away from him. "Are you laughing at me?"

Dustin's expression instantly sobered. She wouldn't look at him, so he used his finger to turn her chin so his gaze could meet hers. "I would never do that."

"No? What, then?" She didn't sound as if she believed him, and she was pulling away from him again, looking anywhere but at his face.

"You're just so sweet," he admitted after a long pause, and trying to choose his words with care. "What can I say?"

"Sweet?"

To Dustin's surprise, she looked genuinely offended, cocking her hands on her hips and glaring back at him as if he'd just called her a bad name.

What had he said?

At least she was looking at him again, he supposed, approaching the issue with his usual humor.

"Sweet?" she repeated, her voice an octave higher than usual. "Dustin James Fairfax, I may be many things, but *sweet* is definitely not one of them."

Dustin shoved his hands in his pockets and pulled his shoulders in tight. When she used his middle name like that she sounded like his mother.

"Sorry," he said, not quite contrite but refusing to admit it. He wondered how he was going to manage six weeks with this woman.

And they called *him* flighty.

"Well?" She stood frozen in the same intimidating position, staring him down.

If she was trying to make him feel smaller, it wasn't working. She wasn't going to intimidate him, no matter what she did.

He wouldn't let her. A lifetime of intimidation had made him strong against those kinds of tactics.

She was still staring at him.

"*Well* what?" he snapped, getting tired of all her wily female games. He'd given her a compliment, after all. What was the big deal?

She remained silent, continuing to stare at him as if he'd grown an extra nose.

"Are you waiting for me to take it back?" he asked, his voice gruff. "Because if you are, you'll be waiting for eternity."

And even then he wasn't sure he was going to be ready to concede, he thought mulishly, crossing his arms over his chest.

She sighed loudly and rolled her eyes. "What I *want* is an explanation."

"Oh, that," he said as if he'd moved long past the scene she'd just witnessed, though now that he was really looking at her he could see her head was still spinning from the encounter.

"Yes," she said blithely, imitating his tone, which he now realized sounded faintly temperamental. "*That.* I take it you do *that* often?"

He shrugged noncommittally. He hadn't really given his actions much thought, other than that they helped another human being. Wasn't that what everyone did? "I get out when I can."

"Well, I think that's spectacular." Her expression told him more than her words could have done. She looked at him as if he were truly someone special.

He turned to her and grasped her gently by the elbows. Her eyes were shining in the soft twilight and his heart was beating double time. No one had ever looked at him that way before. "Do you really think so?"

"Dustin, that was incredible. Remarkable. *You* were remarkable."

"No, Isobel, I'm not. I'm just a man. I do what I can," he repeated again. He felt like squirming under her intense scrutiny and had the feeling she was looking at him like some kind of superhero or something.

"Why did you give her that piece of paper?" she asked quietly. "I don't mean to pry, so feel free not to answer if you don't feel comfortable in doing so. I thought it might be for food or something. Dinner."

"A French dinner," he corrected with a laugh, shaking his head at her expression.

"Even more intriguing."

"Well, I'd have bought her a bag of groceries, but what would she do with it?" His hands slid up her arms to her shoulders. "She doesn't have a microwave or a refrigerator."

Isobel's expression was so melancholy he wanted to hug her, but he didn't know her well enough to fold her in his arms. His words would have to do, though that didn't seem like nearly enough.

The harsh reality was that he couldn't save Rosalinda, he could only be her friend.

"I can't just give her money, Isobel. She'll buy a bottle of liquor with it. That's a fact."

Isobel shivered despite the fact the evening was warm for winter in Colorado. The old woman had been so sweet, so fragile. And yet the reality was she was a homeless alcoholic.

"She's made her own choices," Dustin

said firmly, taking Isobel by the shoulders and gently brushing his palms down her upper arms. He felt her shiver, and knew it wasn't the brisk night air.

"We can help, but we can't change her ways unless she wants to change. Right now, Rosalinda isn't ready for that kind of commitment. All we can do is give her what she's willing to take, and maybe in some subtle way keep tabs on her to make sure she's okay.

"A friend of mine owns a restaurant and has a heart for the homeless. It's a fancy, high-class French joint. I'll have to take you there sometime for dinner. The food is delicious. I think you'd like it."

Isobel brushed over what almost sounded like an invitation. A date. But, of course, that was ridiculous. She was working for him — or rather, his brother.

A date with Dustin was out of the question. So why did it sound so appealing?

"And he seats the homeless people right in the middle of the dining area? Wouldn't they feel uncomfortable in such a setting?" she asked in disbelief. "Not to mention the guests."

"Not he. She. Linda."

Isobel didn't outwardly react to the news that Dustin's friend was a woman, but she couldn't deny the internal tug of disappointment — or was that jealousy? — she experienced upon hearing the information.

He paused, his fingers playing with the curl on his forehead. "And she already had in mind what you were saying. In fact, she built a special room for the comfort of the homeless."

He was impressed that Isobel had thought of Rosalinda's comfort first, rather than the rich patrons who usually frequented the restaurant.

As if suddenly realizing his grip on Isobel had tightened, Dustin suddenly dropped his arms and stepped back, clasping his hands behind his back and clearing his throat. With a light smile, he began walking down the street, nodding his head for her to follow.

He didn't look back to see if she was behind him or not, but assumed she would keep pace with him, as she had all evening.

He was wrong.

Isobel narrowed her gaze on his back, her hands on her hips. "You haven't told Addison about this little hobby of yours, have you?"

He froze midstep, his back and shoulders turning rigid.

"That's what I thought," she said, taking

his posture as an answer.

"Don't even think about it," he said, his tone low and tense. "I didn't bring you with me today to show off to you, Belle. I don't want Addison knowing a thing about what just happened."

Isobel smiled softly at Dustin's pet name for her. She had no idea where he'd dreamed it up, but for some reason she liked it — though, if the moniker were to come from someone's lips other than Dustin's, she was sure she'd be mortified.

Stepping forward to catch up with him, she laid a reassuring hand on his arm. He had to know she respected his motives. How could she not? He had the gallantry of a medieval knight.

But if his brother knew of his compassion for the homeless, wouldn't that be a big plus in his favor of getting the trust fund? Dustin might not have to endure these six weeks with her if he only came clean with what he did in his spare time.

It just didn't make sense to her.

"Dustin, I would never do anything without your permission, but I really think Addison's opinion of your *contribution to society* would change if he could see you with Rosalinda — and all those other homeless people I suspect have been touched by your good heart. Don't you think it would be worth a try?"

"That would ruin everything," he snapped tersely. "Stay out of it."

Isobel knew the stress Dustin's older brother was putting on him was starting to wear thin. She could see the strain in his expression. And yet for a long moment, he didn't speak.

She stayed quiet, patiently waiting for the explanation she sensed was forthcoming. She'd not known him long, but she knew him enough already to know he had his own reasons for doing things; he wasn't exactly conventional in his methods.

Eventually, Dustin sighed and she sensed the tension slowly easing from his body. He clenched his fists for a moment, and then gradually released them.

Finally, he turned to look at her, his gaze warm and tender, his arms stretched toward her, almost pleading as he approached her.

"Sorry, Isobel, I don't mean to take it out on you. I shouldn't have been so irritable." He shrugged his shoulders. "This whole money thing is a bit much sometimes, but I shouldn't take it out on you. Sometimes I just want to punch something, you know? Like a brick wall?"

"I can't even begin to imagine," she said

earnestly, placing a hand over her heart as a gesture of sincerity.

"I mean, I know you're right in one sense," he said thoughtfully. "That if I told Addison about Rosalinda, he might be more inclined to release the funds to me."

He took a deep, steadying breath and shook his head. "I would have all this money to use to build a homeless shelter or something."

He paused a moment, jamming both hands into his already untidy hair. "There's just something that feels *wrong* about telling Addison."

Isobel nodded. "But when you do a charitable deed, do not let your left hand know what your right hand is doing, that your charitable deed may be in secret; and your Father who sees in secret will Himself reward you openly."

"Matthew 6:3–4," Dustin choked out. "So you're a Christian, then. I thought you might be."

She nodded. "I taught my fifth- and sixth-grade Sunday school class that verse last year." She smiled at the memory.

"A Sunday school teacher, huh?" He winked at her. "You sure don't look like any Sunday school teacher I know. I probably would have gone to church more often as a kid if I'd had a teacher as pretty as you."

She blushed a bright, becoming pink, though Dustin had only been voicing an opinion he'd had since the moment he'd first seen her in the deli.

"Well," he said, deciding to have mercy on poor Isobel, who was hemming and hawing and squirming. "At least you get what I'm trying to do here."

He watched as she slowly calmed down, and he was perplexed. She obviously wasn't used to compliments, yet she was a beautiful woman, inside and out.

It gave him pause to wonder what her past had been like.

At length, she smiled at him. "And here I am, standing here staring at you like a constant reminder of your trouble. Like a porcupine rubbing against you."

"A porcupine?" he repeated, in a high, stilted voice, sounding stunned.

He turned and looked her over with an amused grin, his eyes twinkling with merriment. "I don't *think* so. Not in a million years."

"But it bothers you to have me here," she hinted without the least bit of subtlety. She wasn't about to mince words now.

"No," he answered definitively. "You, my dear Isobel, are the best thing that has happened to me in a long time. Maybe ever," he added in a quiet undertone.

He looked away from her, suddenly studying the still busy activity of the street.

Isobel felt a choking sensation at his words, and became even more emotional when his gaze suddenly turned back to her and she stared into the sincere brightness of his eyes.

Eyes that pleaded with her to understand, to walk with him in this one thing.

And how could she do less?

He was so real, so in the moment, that it almost frightened her, more now than at any other time since she'd been with him.

"But you won't tell," he said softly, again looking away from her, stuffing his hands in the pockets of his jeans in a gesture she now recognized as a subtle form of anxiety in the most carefree man she'd ever known.

It was just another incongruity in Dustin Fairfax, another puzzle Isobel meant to solve before her six weeks were over.

She heard the catch in his voice and knew his words were a question, though he'd artfully phrased it as a statement.

"No," she assured him, her voice suddenly unable to go above a whisper. "I won't tell."

CHAPTER SEVEN

Dustin arrived at the Regency Oak Towers in the Denver Technical Center shortly after 5:00 p.m. Dressed in his usual jeans, T-shirt and a bomber jacket, he felt a little uncomfortable entering the flashy hotel lobby.

He cringed at the very thought of the time, because five *sharp* was when Isobel was expecting him, and he knew exactly what that fact meant for him.

He was gonna get chewed.

It was her job, after all. Miss Perfectionist, with her intimidating habit of constantly looking at her watch, a habit he doubted she even noticed.

With Isobel, Dustin knew, even a minute late was *late,* and he was at least ten minutes behind — maybe more, with the way his life tended to run.

He didn't know the exact time because he forgot to wear a watch.

Okay, so he didn't *own* a watch. But what

was a little semantics between friends?

Isobel would consider it showing his true colors, and it would no doubt make the *image consultant* part of her wish to give him the tongue-lashing he so richly deserved by his actions.

Dustin found it amusing to think of Isobel this way, on a high horse and full of righteous indignation . . . as long as it wasn't aimed right at him.

He chuckled under his breath. Whether or not she followed through on her career-focused instincts remained to be seen.

Would she take him to task on a few measly lost minutes?

The Tech Center, the major business hub in Denver, was surrounded by huge international firms and was the centerpiece for out-of-town business. Thus, a number of high-end hotels with excellent service and gigantic conference rooms to service their affluent and prestigious clientele were at virtually every corner of the complex, each vying for the upscale business.

Wishing not for the first time he'd picked up one of those five-dollar, big-faced watches at a discount store as he had considered doing for Isobel's sake, he pushed through the highly polished revolving glass doors and made his way into the hotel.

He really did hate watches — they made him too aware of time. They made him tense and stressed when he didn't want to be — and especially when he needed to be at his best.

Like now. And he was *late.*

At least he could have brought Isobel a bouquet of flowers to ease the way into her good graces. He owned a flower shop, after all. He hadn't even considered the obvious.

How dumb was that?

He was still pondering his error when he was hailed by a bouncy, lively Camille, who looked like — by her hair and the way she flittered around — she'd had a few too many double-shot espressos. Dustin had never met her in person but Isobel had described her with remarkably accurate detail, right down to the Irish red hair.

She was waiting for him behind the concierge desk. Her palm drummed out a nervous rhythm on the desk and she sang softly with the beat she had created, all the time waving to him with her other hand.

"Dustin," she called sharply as he wandered aimlessly through the lobby. She continued her energetic arm movements, waving over her head so there was no way he could possibly have missed her.

He removed his ball cap and scratched the top of his head. His gaze remained on Camille as he smiled a bemused hello.

"Dustin Fairfax. You're just the way I pictured you." Her voice was a rich, vibrant alto, bouncy and full of life. Quite a contrast to Isobel's soft, high voice, Dustin mused.

He nodded.

"She filled me in on every detail of what has happened to you so far. For what it's worth, your hair looks great. I heard all about it — Ricardo is really something, isn't he? He does my hair — but I'm not afraid to tell you I was scared out of my wits when Isobel first recommended him. As long as the guy does his job well, though, don't you know what I mean?"

Dustin didn't have an opinion on the issue — he only wondered if he would be allowed to get a word in edgewise if he did. Camille was like a machine gun; her words shooting out so quickly he couldn't make heads or tails of any of them.

This was something Isobel hadn't mentioned when she'd told him all about her best friend. She'd obviously told Camille more about him than she'd told him about her closest friend and roommate.

Camille continued to prattle on, waving

111

her hands enthusiastically as she spoke. "Isobel wasn't fibbing when she called you the next major hunk to take Denver by storm."

The woman didn't seem the least bit embarrassed or shy about her statements. It wasn't that she appeared a ditz, not aware of what she was saying, and blathering on and on about everything. Rather, her soliloquy appeared to be a clear-cut judgment of how she saw things in the world. No blushing or pandering with Camille, just an honest assessment, straight up.

He kind of liked it, and immediately saw how Camille complemented Isobel. It gave him insight into why they had become fast friends.

He already liked this happy, carefree woman who was Isobel's best friend from childhood, and thought he understood why Isobel shared such a close-knit bond with such a happy, outgoing person.

"Did Isobel really say that about me?" he queried, his grin widening.

Camille barked out a laugh. "Ha! You know Izzy better than that by now — or at least I hope you do!" she said, waving her hands in denial.

"She'd never say anything like that — not in so many words, anyway. But Izzy is the best image consultant in the industry, if I do say so myself — and I do. You can bet by the time she's through with you, you'll be just exactly what I said you will be — the next major hunk to hit the Denver area."

Dustin replaced his cap. "I don't know about that," he replied, honestly but not warily. "Isobel's been good for me, that's for sure."

Camille eyed him with intelligent, amused, interested green eyes. "Do you think?" She laughed heartily at her rhetorical question.

He answered it anyway, nodding vigorously. "Yeah. I sure do."

"I'm Camille, by the way. Isobel's best friend. She told you about me?"

Dustin laughed. "She told you about me, didn't she?" he queried.

"Well, yes. She tells me everything, of course. You're just —"

Dustin cut her off. "A hopelessly backward male who needs some refinement?" he offered.

Camille laughed with delight. "I like you. I really like you."

"I like you, too," Dustin said honestly.

His mind brushed quickly over the details he knew about Isobel's friend.

Camille had joined Isobel in pursuing their higher education in Denver from some kind of Texas backwoods childhood, choosing a career in the hospitality arts, whereas Isobel had pursued the fashion industry. With Camille's bubbly, open personality it was no wonder she was a successful businesswoman, having risen to assistant concierge of one of the most prestigious hotels in the metro area.

"I think you'd better get up there," Camille said. "Isobel is anxiously waiting for your arrival."

"*Anxious* being the key word," Dustin said, groaning. He lifted an eyebrow. "Up where, exactly?"

"Fifth floor. It's the second conference room to the left."

"Got it. Thanks for the help. And it was nice meeting you, Camille." He fingered the rim of his cap and tipped his head.

"Oh, no," Camille protested with a friendly wink. "The pleasure is all mine. I hope we see each other again soon."

"I'm sure we will," he responded politely, his mind already half on what was to come.

Actually, he wasn't exactly sure what *was* to come. But he had more pressing matters at the moment.

He wasn't too fond of the glass elevator that skimmed its way up and down the exterior of the hotel, but the view of brightly lit downtown Denver in the dusky twilight was almost worth the way his stomach turned upside down as he rose floor by floor.

Almost. He didn't especially like heights — particularly in see-through elevators.

He was most heartily relieved to reach the fifth floor, and he quickly stepped out onto the firmness of the hotel floor, letting out a deep breath as his feet touched the solid, unmoving floor.

Staring at the beckoning door to the conference room, he ran his tongue across his dry lips and sighed deeply, then removed his ball cap and stuffed it into the back pocket of his jeans.

The things he was willing to do for a trust fund.

Dustin thought the convention room he entered must be the hotel's largest, for it had effectively been transformed into a fashion runway.

Isobel had said the hotel would be the location of a prestigious spring fashion show, but he had never expected an actual *runway.* Not in the middle of a conference room more suited for, well, *conferences.*

There was a small, gold-curtained stage near the back, obviously constructed just for the event. The chairs for the guests had been assembled in straight rows around the runway and were draped in shimmering strips of gold.

The only thing missing from the sparkling picture was Isobel.

Dustin shoved his hands into his bomber jacket pockets and just stared at the spectacle for a moment, taking it all in and feeling a tight, cold fist in the bottom of his gut.

This was where Isobel belonged, amongst all this glitz and glamour. For a moment, he thought he might have caught a glimpse of her heart.

But shimmering and gold was all that Dustin was not. If she was thinking to change him into this, she would have to think again.

"What's wrong?" Isobel asked, having come up from behind him and noticing his low brow and the stubborn set of his chin. "You look like your dog just ate your ice-cream cone."

He jumped back like a kid caught with both hands in the cookie jar.

"What's wrong?" she asked again, patiently looking up at him.

Dustin's features evened out, settling into his usual cheerful countenance. "Nothing's wrong. You just startled me."

"I don't believe you," she said frankly as

she met his guilty-eyed gaze, and felt a little hurt at his reticence to confide. "But I'm not going to push you into telling me what you were really thinking."

He gave a dry laugh. "I thought that was your job — pushing me around."

She felt heat rush to her cheeks and knew Dustin would be able to see the result of his teasing on her reddened face, if teasing was indeed what he had meant by his remark. He had sounded quite serious, and his expression gave nothing away. She didn't know whether to laugh or cry.

Deciding to ignore his unsettling comment, she changed the topic. "Well, I'm glad you're here," she said in as light a tone as she was able. "We have a lot to do this evening, and we need to get started right away if we're going to accomplish anything."

"Do?" Dustin stiffened. "I was hoping you were going to say you just wanted to give me a tour of this place. You know, show me the ropes of what you do around here."

She lifted an eyebrow.

"I'm interested in what you do for a living," he insisted, giving her his best cheeky grin. "This is all new to me."

"Trust me," Isobel purred. "I'm going to *show you the ropes.*"

Dustin narrowed his gaze on her, his green

eyes gleaming with amusement. "I've heard that tune before," he reminded her in a dry, suspicious tone.

Isobel laughed gaily, curving her arm through his. "Come on. I promise this won't hurt nearly as much as your haircut did. It's nothing permanent or irreversible. Who knows — you might even like it."

He snorted. "Famous last words. I notice you didn't say it wasn't going to hurt, only *not as much.* What am I supposed to take from that?"

She frantically pulled in the smile that threatened to crease her face from ear to ear. Dustin needn't know how funny and boyish his expression looked as she purposefully goaded him.

She leaned into his arm, running a delicate hand across his biceps. "Never tell me a big, strong man like you will let something as harmless as a new set of clothes scare him."

"Clothes?" he choked out, pulling down on the rim of his ball cap. "That definitely has the same ring to it as *haircut.*"

Isobel laughed again and continued to pull him forward toward the stage. "C'mon, big boy, and let me introduce you to a couple of my good friends, Jon and Robert. I'm sure you'll like them."

Dustin threw her another suspicious look.

"Who are Jon and Robert?"

"They work in the industry. You should feel honored. These guys are giving us their time for free as a favor to me."

"Oh, joy," he said, with just a touch of sarcasm lining his voice.

Isobel sniffed, letting him know she was offended by his candid remark. "They happen to be top-of-the-line experts — the very talented and creative assistants of Wanda Warner."

He shook his head, his gaze letting her know the name didn't ring a bell. "And she would be . . . ?"

"Oh, *please* don't tell me you've never heard of the most popular western clothing designer on two continents. I'll be mortally offended if you do."

He shrugged. "Sorry. No."

He didn't sound sorry.

He sounded amused.

She wanted to shake him. What planet was the man living on that he had never heard of Wanda? She was always appearing on the news and specialty television shows, and her face regularly turned up in local and national newspapers.

She even had her own television shopping network that was shown worldwide.

It was almost as if Dustin purposefully

kept himself distanced from the world — a virtual hermit if not a literal one. Did he not even read the daily paper?

"Well, you're about to be introduced," she said firmly, earning a groan from Dustin. "And, please, Dustin, try to be nice to them," she added, remembering their encounter with Ricardo the hairdresser. "It will go easier on you in the end."

It was a veiled threat, and he groaned again, rubbing his forehead with his palm.

She set her face in a businesslike expression, unwilling to let Dustin take the enjoyment out of what was most certainly — at least for her — going to be a fun and extraordinary evening.

Grabbing him by the hand, she tugged him toward the stage, up three steps onto the platform and eventually through the sparkling gold curtain to the back, where her colleagues were waiting.

She was totally aware Dustin was literally dragging his feet, scuffing along like a boy on his way to the dentist's office, but for the moment she chose to ignore his antics and stall tactics. "Jon, Robert, come meet your designated project for this evening."

She felt him pull back again, slamming on the mental brakes, so to speak; but she didn't feel entirely guilty at provoking him.

Jon and Robert were obviously twins, aged somewhere in their mid-twenties. They had polished good looks, but were not the least conservative in their dress. Their clothes were colorful and loud, if carefully coordinated, and definitely western, right down to polished snakeskin cowboy boots.

Isobel knew Dustin wasn't used to working with highflyers like these.

Still, he could be just a little more of a willing participant, in her opinion. He had, after all, agreed to this arrangement between the two of them in the first place. He was the one who would benefit from it in the long run, if he would just give her half a chance, instead of fighting with her every step of the way.

It wasn't exactly as if she were going to be drawing blood.

Dustin surprised her by releasing her hand and offering a firm handshake to each of the two young men in turn.

"Glad to meet you fellows," he said with none of the reticence or patronization she expected. "I hear you've got plans in store for me."

The two men looked at each other and then back at Dustin, breaking into friendly grins.

She wasn't sure if it was a blessing or a

curse that Dustin appeared to have decided to trust her and had capitulated in his attitude.

Finally, he was submitting to her plans with the good grace he usually showed. The night-and-day difference astonished Isobel.

"What's going on here tonight? A fashion show?" Dustin asked, smiling down at her in that quirky way of his that at once conveyed his unspoken apology for his earlier behavior and sent Isobel's heart leaping into her throat, beating a quick, sharp, patent rhythm that she was beginning to recognize as uniquely pursuant to Dustin's warm smile.

It was Dustin's signature on her heart.

He could really be charming when he wanted to be, and right now, he was laying it on full force.

"The fashion show isn't until later this week," Jon said, leaning casually against the nearest wall and crossing his feet at the ankles. "You oughtta ask Isobel to get you a ticket. Five-star event, but our Isobel has that kind of clout, you know."

Dustin cocked an eyebrow and looked down at her, his expression unreadable. "No, I didn't know that about Belle. Not that it surprises me," he continued softly, chuckling under his breath.

Isobel shrugged, feeling uncomfortable with the attention the three men were paying her. To the last man they were staring at her with pride, the younger guys with a touch of envy, and it made her uncomfortable.

"I'm sure you'd really enjoy it, Dustin," Jon said, kindly taking the focus off of her, and not a moment too soon. She'd been on the verge of turning and running. She grinned at him, silently thanking him for rescuing her.

Dustin stiffened, his face screwed into a ball of lines. Isobel realized he was holding back a laugh.

"I'm sure I would," he said in a blithe tone Isobel hoped Jon and Robert wouldn't recognize. "Our Isobel is full to bursting with ideas on how to spruce me up, make me another man."

She knew exactly what he was implying with every word he spoke, so she not so gently laid her heel down on his toes in silent warning, leaning back until she was certain he felt it.

He'd *better* feel it. The cad!

Next time she would stomp.

"What we're doing tonight is kind of like a fashion show," Robert offered, brushing a hand through his curly mop of hay-colored hair.

Isobel gave a small, startled shake of her head to warn the young man off, but the damage had already been done.

"And by that you mean?" Dustin asked warily, looking around at the three of them.

"You'll see," Isobel said, just the littlest bit too brightly.

To her assistants, she merely said, "Guys, why don't we get started?"

Chapter Eight

"Jon and Robert, as I briefed you earlier, and as you can now obviously see for yourself, my client needs a fashion makeover in a mean way."

She cringed inside. She had almost said *friend,* and deep down she knew it was true. Dustin was very much becoming a friend.

But she had to keep her professional boundaries, not get her priorities mixed up. She had a job to do. He was her client — and that was only for what was left of the six weeks they would spend together.

"I'm *mean?*" Dustin queried, raising both his eyebrows. Isobel had opened herself up for it, and he just couldn't resist teasing her about it.

"I hope that's not meant to be literal, Belle." He grinned at Isobel and winked.

She held a straight face, but he could see the sides of her lips twitching. "Wait and see, Fairfax."

She clapped her hands twice. "Jon and Robert, let's get started."

Started, Dustin soon discovered, was trying on an inordinate number of outfits — slacks, dress shirts, jeans, casual shirts — even shoes! More clothes than he'd ever seen — or *wanted* to see — in his whole life. Where did they get all these things?

But the three fashion moguls in his company were undaunted, and continued to send him back and forth from the dressing room with new sets of outfits. They commented amongst themselves at each new combination of garments, but didn't let him hear a word until Isobel was ready to proclaim her final opinion.

And the tuxedos, sports coats, and hats.

So many different kinds of hats! There was an entire rack of them!

He was given baseball caps — which he didn't mind too much; felt fedoras that, in his opinion, made him look like a gangster out of the 1920s; and even one top hat which, he had to admit, looked pretty classy.

Even on him.

There were so many clothes, and he quickly found he would have the unfortunate experience of putting on and taking off every single item.

It wasn't exactly his first choice for a night

out. Not even in the ballpark.

And his feet were beginning to hurt from some *very* uncomfortable oxfords squeezing his toes together.

"Oh, now *that* is a nice look," Isobel commented on one particular outfit, making her opinion known as she had on every other. "It's casual, yet it lends the distinction of class."

Dustin stared in the three-way mirror, shaking his head in astonishment. For once, he couldn't formulate the words to tell her how he felt.

Maybe it was because his brain had turned into a speeding highway, one thought after the next threatening to collide with one another. He couldn't find room in his mind to make audible speech.

The tight indigo-blue designer jeans they'd given him were all right, he supposed, though in truth he much preferred his jeans loose and well-worn.

But a pink shirt?

It was a nice, snap-down dress shirt, made of extra-soft material Dustin couldn't identify. It fit his broad shoulders perfectly and tapered to his waist, where he tucked it into his pants.

In other circumstances — or more precisely, other colors — Dustin would have been impressed by the shirt, maybe even have worn it, despite the western look to it he wasn't real keen on.

But pink?

No way.

Not on this man.

"It's gorgeous," Isobel proclaimed, clapping her hands together in sheer delight.

"It's awful," Dustin replied instantly, cutting her off before she could rant and rave some more.

"And I'm taking it off. Now."

He made good on his threat and began unsnapping the shirt, not even bothering to go back into his dressing room to do so.

"But Dustin!" she protested, slapping her palms over her cheeks as he peeled off the shirt right in front of her.

"I draw the line at *pink*, Isobel," he said, trying to keep his voice sober, though he knew a gleam of amusement must have shown from his eyes. He wasn't really angry as much as annoyed.

How could she think he would be the kind of man who would wear pink? He wasn't *that* comfortable with his masculinity.

Deep down, he wondered how much she really knew about him, when she couldn't even pick out appropriate colors for him to wear, colors that matched his lifestyle and personality.

It seemed to be the sort of thing an image consultant ought to know instinctively, and especially after spending some time together with him.

"But it looks good on you," she protested again in a gravelly tone, moving her hands to her hips. "Spectacular, even."

"You have got to be kidding." He wasn't going to argue about this.

"You are so closed-minded," she retorted, angrily stepping forward to face him.

"Mebbe," he growled low in his throat. "But I," he informed her through gritted teeth, "will never, ever wear anything *pink*."

He paused for effect.

"Not a pink shirt, not pink pants, not pink shoes and not a pink hat," he said, feeling as if he were quoting something from Dr. Seuss. "I won't even wear pink pajamas, thank you very much. So can we please move on to another subject? Like *blue*?"

Isobel let out a loud huff of breath as Jon and Robert, whom Dustin had mentally tagged *Riff* and *Raff,* chuckled under their breath.

"Some people's children," Isobel muttered irritably as she turned to find something new on the wardrobe rack. She pushed the clothes hangers around loud enough to make sure every one of the men in her presence knew she *meant* to stir up a ruckus.

"What was that?" Dustin queried, chuckling and raising an eyebrow.

"Nothing," she snapped, keeping her back to him and continuing to riffle through the clothes.

"You mean nothing I'd want to know about," he corrected casually.

She whirled around and glared at him, her eyes spitting fire. "Whatever."

Dustin knew then that he'd really offended her, and he took the offensive to make it right with her again, submitting to the ministrations of Riff and Raff and cracking jokes that made the men, at least, loosen up and laugh a little bit.

But it took another long, excruciating hour before Isobel finally settled on an outfit that both pleased her and that Dustin didn't whine about.

"You are so lucky," she informed him, her tone still a little sharp and exasperated. "Do you know how many men can get away with pleated slacks with cuffs, and actually look good in them?"

He rolled his eyes but then grinned in her direction, trying to ease the tension between the two of them but still not ready to give in to her demands. "No, Belle. Tell me."

Either she didn't hear the irony in his voice or she was ignoring it. Or maybe her answer would have been the same either way.

"Close to none," she said crisply, brushing her palms together as if brushing off any rebuttals he might have made.

"Honestly," she continued before he could speak, "so many men wear pleats and shouldn't. You need broad shoulders to balance the look, and of course a trim, tight torso."

Dustin grinned and patted his stomach. "Three hundred sit-ups each and every morning, first thing. Guess it's done the trick."

"Evidently," she said wryly, looking anywhere but at him.

He chuckled.

"Besides you, Dustin, I can only think of one man who really does those pants justice, and he's a television hunk."

Both of Dustin's eyebrows hit his hairline at her words and his mouth dropped open.

"Hunk?" he teased.

She brushed his comment off and kept her eyes carefully averted. Isobel didn't want to be thinking about his nice physique right now, unless it was related to the clothes she wanted him to wear.

"Whatever."

Truth be told, the real hunk was standing before her, and despite their differences in opinion over fashion styles and what he should wear, she knew she was succumbing to his innate charm.

He was one of those men who didn't have the slightest idea what they had going for them — which was just as well. He'd be a dangerous, and no doubt arrogant, man if he knew the effect he had on women.

On her.

She mentally shook herself out of her emotional relapse. She still had work to do, and she wouldn't let her latent feelings for Dustin keep her from getting the job done.

Without a single word to him, she held out her hand to him.

He took it without comment and allowed himself to be pulled through the golden stage curtain and on to the runway.

"This is very important, Dustin, so please try to follow my instructions to the letter." Her voice was low and crisp.

"Yes, ma'am," he replied with a playful salute. "Whatever you say."

"Spotlights, Jon," she called loudly. Immediately a hot, bright spotlight put Dustin and Isobel at the center of the action.

"Spotlights?" Dustin queried warily, dropping her hand. Something was up, and he wanted to know what it was. "What's with the spotlights?"

"You'll understand in a minute, hon," Isobel said with a short laugh.

"Why do I think I'm not going to like this?" he asked wryly, lifting his left eyebrow. His muscles tensed as if in preparation for the worst.

"Oh, it won't hurt. I promise."

Dustin just shook his head.

"It's that simple, really. All I want you to do is put on some attitude. Be your usual confident self, only with a little punch."

"And?" he asked. It sounded as if he might be gritting his teeth, and Isobel well knew she was gritting hers.

He wasn't going to like this.

"And," Isobel continued, half holding her breath, "I want you to walk down to the end of the runway, turn around as if there were big crowds of fashion-conscious magazine editors out there in those chairs watching you, and then walk back to the curtain."

She paused. This was an important moment. If she couldn't get him to comply in this one area, to show off the confidence she believed he possessed, then it would be all uphill from here.

How else would she ever begin to get him

up to snuff for the really important moments, when people would be present?

Watching him. Judging him.

"Nothing could be simpler, Dustin. It might be fun, even." Her voice cracked, and she wondered if he noticed the slight lapse.

"Not a chance," Dustin informed her in a deep, slow, firm monotone voice that indicated he would brook no argument.

"I'm not asking you to do anything illegal," Isobel retorted, mild anger showing in her tone despite her best efforts. She'd known this wasn't going to be easy, but she'd hoped for the best, despite it all.

He grunted.

"What could be easier than walking the runway? No one is here to see you but me."

"Don't forget Riff and Raff," he pointed out, crossing his arms and sounding just a bit like a pouting child, at least to Isobel. "And as for the runway, I can tell you right now I would look like an idiot strutting around like that, showing off some dumb clothes."

He looked at her then, his gaze pleading in a way his words could never do. He looked as if he were in pain, and it struck right at her heart.

After a moment, he groaned. "Don't ask me to do this, Isobel. It isn't me."

She wanted to let him off the hook. Her heart was screaming to give the poor man a break.

But this was for his own good, she reminded herself. He needed to do this, needed to see what it felt like under the spotlight.

"Please?" She was begging now, and they both knew it. "For me?"

He shook his head, but at the same time stepped forward and onto the runway, glowering down at her from his new height. "Very well," he said, his voice tight. "For you."

With a frown, he started down the runway. It wasn't long before Isobel detected his intentions weren't entirely honest. Fire and ice fought inside her as she watched him make a mockery of her life, and his chances of getting the trust-fund money.

It began subtly, with a turn of his hips and an occasional hand flipping in the air in an unusually cocked manner. Then he started strutting and jerking all the way down the aisle.

The only sound was the click and thump of the boots he was wearing with the outfit Isobel had devised. It didn't take a neurosurgeon to figure out he was doing a man's imitation of a female runway model.

Poorly.

For Isobel, it was the last straw.

She threw down the clipboard she was holding and let it clatter to the floor.

The noise stopped Dustin in his tracks, though he didn't turn and look at her.

"That's it," she said, unable to keep the anger and frustration she was feeling from her voice. Rage surged through her in hot waves.

And the worst part was she didn't care. "You want to change, Dustin Fairfax, do it yourself. At this moment, I couldn't care less about you, your brother's crazy ideas or the money in your stupid trust fund."

She drew in a large, loud breath and glared at his back. "I quit."

It was the first sensible thing she had said all day — maybe for weeks, she thought to herself. It was as if a weight was lifted from her shoulders, now that the stress of the situation was gone.

And the sooner she got away from Dustin Fairfax, the better.

She turned and hiked toward the door, not daring to look back to see what Dustin was doing.

"Isobel," he roared, and she froze solid in the spot despite her best efforts to keep moving.

Every bone in her body screamed for her to run, but there seemed to be a short between her brain and her limbs. She couldn't move a muscle.

"Turn around." His hard voice was a command, and she knew she should be offended, but she didn't move.

She couldn't.

"Isobel, please."

The tender, genuine ache in his voice as he spoke moved her heart as no cold command could have.

She didn't stride off in indignation.

She turned.

If his genuine honesty had compelled her to stop and turn around, it was the hopeful pleading in his wide green eyes that made her stay.

"Belle, look at me," he said, his voice low and hypnotic. "Just stand there a moment more and watch me. Please."

How could she not?

She was mesmerized by him. His every move was slow and calculated, and graceful in the way of a large wildcat in its mountain home.

Slowly, sweat dripping unheeded from his forehead, step by excruciating step, he walked down the runway, putting every effort into transforming himself into the poised and well-postured man Belle wanted him to be.

He exceeded every aspect of a true runway model. His male ego would settle for nothing less. His boots made no sound this time as he glided along; all she could hear was his labored breathing.

No swaying hips or obnoxious comments in a falsetto voice followed these movements, and she was overwhelmed by the pull of his will alone.

He was sleek, smooth and oh, so masculine, in a way none of the male models of her acquaintance could even remotely simulate. His face was a study in strong lines and smooth planes as the lights teased his shadowed expression and his concentrated steps.

After what seemed an excruciatingly long time, Dustin reached the end of the runway and paused. Electricity crackled in the air.

Isobel held her breath in unconscious anticipation, thinking he might do something boyish and silly and totally Dustin to ruin the moment — something like taking a running leap off the constructed platform and screaming like a banshee all the way down.

And yet . . .

He broke for only one moment in order

to flash her a cheeky grin that made her heart skip a beat. Then he was absolute model material again, as he carefully removed his sports coat and, with a beautifully executed turn that reminded her more of a dancer than a model, turned back toward the stage, flipping the jacket with casual ease onto his shoulder.

With another smooth turn he stepped confidently to the end of the runway and pulled at the silk tie, then unbuttoned the top button of the rose-pink shirt he vowed he'd never wear in public.

Pink or no pink, the man oozed masculinity.

When he was finished with his spotless routine, he gave a subtle, after-work casualness to his overall appearance, like he'd finished his workday and was just beginning to relax and kick back.

Isobel had never seen anything like the performance Dustin Fairfax was giving her right now.

Everything from his confident male swagger to the stray lock of hair that fell over his forehead was as professional as it was endearing. She swallowed hard, forcing herself to keep breathing, to keep watching this magnificent sight. She was certain she'd never see anything quite like this again.

Dustin pivoted once more and walked back up the runway until he disappeared behind the sparkling gold curtain.

Isobel didn't move, not at all sure what to expect next. She thought perhaps she ought to follow him backstage, but her legs felt like jelly and she wasn't sure she could walk even if she wanted to.

A few moments later, Dustin slid back through the curtain, and Isobel released the breath she hadn't even realized she'd been holding.

The coat was gone, his pink sleeves were rolled up over his elbows, he'd unhitched the second button on his shirt and his baseball cap was back — or more accurately, *backward* — on his head.

He cocked his chin and raised his hands in question, turning around once for her inspection, laughing at his own performance.

Isobel just stared at him, thinking he looked every bit as handsome the way he was now as he did dressed up out of his measure.

Maybe more.

"Well?" he asked when she didn't speak. "Am I forgiven?"

CHAPTER NINE

Isobel supposed she was giving a bit of a peace offering when she showed up at Dustin's door Saturday morning, with a dozen or so new outfits for him in the trunk of her car.

This time she'd included a few casual outfits she hoped he might actually wear, for she now knew Dustin's personality well enough to know he would never really convert to wearing business suits and ties.

That just wasn't Dustin.

That being said, there would be times when he could not avoid wearing a suit, and at the moment, both of them knew this six weeks was in that category. The grand finale was a posh dinner hosted by his brother. Dustin would *have* to dress up for that.

Feeling oddly nervous, she took a deep, cleansing breath and glanced at her watch.

9:00 a.m.

Isobel was a morning person by nature,

and it hadn't occurred to her until this moment, when she was literally standing here on his doorstep, that Dustin might not be.

She wished she'd thought of it earlier.

If Dustin was a night owl and liked to sleep in late, he was not going to appreciate her gesture of goodwill when the sun was still low in the east and bright in the sky.

She hesitated a moment before raising her hand to knock. For a moment, she thought of turning around, leaving and returning later in the day.

But, after all, she was already here, she reasoned, so she might as well go ahead and knock. If he was rumpled and grumpy and growled at her to come back later, she would.

She knocked several times, pounding harder with each effort. She called Dustin's name, thinking he might be deeply involved in some project and, in typical Dustin fashion, had become entirely unaware of the world around him as he worked at whatever it was he was doing.

His ability to lose himself completely in whatever he was doing, working at everything he did with his whole heart, was actually a quality she much admired in him, as she herself was always ultra-aware of her surroundings and what was going on about her, often to the point of distraction.

At this particular moment, however, his tendency to get lost in things was annoying her. She had handpicked the outfits she had with her to give him as a present, and she was going to be very disappointed if he wasn't home or wouldn't answer his door.

She realized in hindsight she probably should have called first as a common courtesy, but she had wanted to make her appearance at his door a complete surprise — hopefully a good one.

Well! She had done that, all right. He was so surprised he wasn't even home.

Crestfallen, she shifted her attention to her surroundings. There were two cars in his driveway. The first was a practical compact car, appropriate for a single man to get around with, she supposed, though in truth a little boring for her perception of Dustin.

The second was a beat-up piece of junk Isobel barely recognized but supposed she would classify as some sort of old-time sports car.

His *sports car!*

Could it be?

She laughed aloud as she looked the car over. She would doubt if the thing even ran, were it not that he'd said he'd had it with him when they first met — offered her a ride, in fact.

Maybe she should have taken him up on it.

She stifled another laugh, but couldn't help the grin that continued to line her face.

So much for first impressions.

With Dustin, nothing was ever what it seemed on the surface. Everything about him was a mystery, and what he offered openly was completely incomprehensible to the normal female mind.

At least hers. But then, she thought wryly, not too many people she knew would classify her as *normal.*

Her curiosity piqued, she stepped around the side of the house and found a Kawasaki motorcycle, every piece of chrome polished to a bright shine, parked against the red-brick wall.

Isobel chuckled. Dustin definitely wasn't a Harley man, but it didn't entirely surprise her to find he tooled around on a motorcycle.

He marched to the beat of his own drummer, that was for certain.

She examined the motorcycle, as she had never actually been this close to one before. It looked a little dangerous, with all those pipes and rods. Her heart beat a little faster.

Suddenly and quite abruptly, she became aware of music.

She froze in place, her ear tuned to discovering the location of the pleasant sound, which she had quickly identified as some form of classical music being played on a piano.

But where was the delightful music coming from?

She couldn't quite place it, and suddenly had an incorrigible need to know. Maybe it was that incomprehensible connection she felt with Dustin. She hadn't known him that long, yet for some reason she thought it might be him, despite the fact that he had never mentioned music, much less played the piano in front of her before.

Was she right? Was it Dustin?

She walked slowly around to the back of Dustin's house, letting herself in through the unlocked picket gate and feeling a little like an intruder prowling about where she didn't belong.

She wasn't sure what Dustin would think of her letting herself into his backyard that way, but once struck, she could not help but continue until her curiosity was met as to where the sound originated.

The music led her on.

She turned the corner of the brick house.

Dustin's backyard was overgrown with weeds from end to end, hadn't been mowed in ages and, most surprising of all, hadn't been landscaped.

Not a single flower bloomed. No color budded from the ground.

And him owning a flower shop.

Dustin was a paradox. An enigma.

And she was more determined than ever to figure him out.

After she had found out where the music was coming from. The longer she listened, the more intrigued she became.

There were sliding glass double doors at the back of Dustin's modest home, and one was open a crack, though the long white drapes were still pulled against the blazing sunlight.

She crept forward, every moment half expecting Dustin to jump out from behind a bush or shrub, shouting "Gotcha" at the top of his lungs and frightening her half out of her wits.

It would be just like Dustin to do that.

But then, who would be playing the piano?

Every nerve on end, she pulled the glass door open mere inches more, only because, she told herself, she now had no doubt whatsoever that the music was coming from within Dustin's house.

Someone was in there playing, and she had to know for certain who it was.

And it was not, she assured herself, any sort of jealousy that led her on, like the unwanted thought that some beautiful woman was in Dustin's house playing on his piano and to his delight.

It was the music and nothing more.

In moments she had confirmed her theory. The piano melody was definitely coming from his house, and she closed her eyes for a moment to savor the warm, familiar classical refrain.

Whoever was playing, he — or she — was good. No, not good.

Gifted.

Hardly knowing she did so, she slid the door half-open so she could slip inside the house. She followed the sound of the music like a tiny mouse at the mercy of the Pied Piper.

Not thinking. Feeling.

She crossed through an empty room that looked as if it served a variety of purposes. There was a computer, a wide workbench with a variety of wood products on it and a table spread with flower cuttings.

Not, she thought with a small smile, flowers fresh from his own garden.

The room had a wood floor that looked as

if it had seen better days. It needed a mop and a good dose of wax, not to mention some elbow grease.

As soon as she hesitantly stepped through the open double doors onto the white shag carpet that covered the next room, she finally located the source of the wonderful music.

Dustin sat straight-backed at a highly polished baby grand, his eyes closed as his fingers flowed effortlessly over the keys.

This room was full of light from the many windows and, unlike the room she'd come from, was fully furnished with what looked like expensive, high-end wood furniture and a posh set of black leather sofas and chairs that looked fabulous against the plush white carpet.

Nicely framed black-and-white art posters lined every wall, placed with a remarkable sense of balance that finished off the room with class and distinction.

Isobel couldn't help the smile that tugged at the corners of her lips. Apparently he hadn't completely lost a sense of his up-bringing.

Suddenly she realized the music had ceased and she froze in place, almost afraid to turn her head in Dustin's direction.

After all, she was, technically, an intruder.

Whether that was a good thing or not was still to be decided.

As much as she would have liked to avoid it, her gaze turned almost of its own consent toward the piano, holding her breath at what she might find there.

Dustin's eyes were open, one eyebrow arched. His arms were crossed over his chest, and his inquiring gaze was upon her.

And that was all.

He didn't even look particularly surprised she had suddenly appeared in his house without being invited. He looked as if he might be wondering *why* she was there, and was only mildly and amusedly curious at discovering the answer to that.

Isobel's face flamed as she realized she *had* no explanation, no rational excuse at all.

She cleared her throat and looked at the floor, stalling for time, though she knew he wouldn't wait forever. She would have to think of some excuse at some point.

Preferably sooner than later.

"Well?" he encouraged, unabashed laughter lining his voice.

"I followed the sound of the music," she blurted at last, then felt her face flame at the weakness of her poor explanation.

He laughed aloud then. "You followed the

music. From your condo in downtown Denver?"

She scowled at him, though in truth she was put out with herself. What kind of fool walked into someone's house uninvited, especially a man she'd only known a short time?

"From your front porch," she answered in a clipped tone. "I dropped by as a surprise to, uh — to give you a present," she stammered.

Dustin's grin disappeared as soon as he heard the word *present.*

A *present?*

Up until this time their acquaintance had been casual, even businesslike, although admittedly he considered her a friend at this point.

He intended to get to know her over these six weeks. He hoped to stay friends with her after his brother's crazy experiment was over.

But still . . .

What had he missed?

Some sort of three week anniversary or such?

It wasn't his birthday.

His male mind scoured the details of their acquaintance for a clue to his oversight and he felt sweat beading on his forehead.

The crux of the matter was that *he* didn't have a present to give to *her.*

He didn't know why it mattered.

She was the one who'd wandered into his house without an invitation, and somehow she'd already turned it around so he was the one pulling at his collar and fidgeting on his piano stool.

Women.

No wonder he was single at thirty.

He'd never understand the female mind, not if he lived to be a hundred.

"Don't look so shocked, Dustin. It's not personal," she said with a chuckle. "It's a professional gift, and your brother paid for it. So you can take a deep breath and relax, cowboy."

Dustin scrunched his face and cringed dramatically. And it wasn't all for show. For one thing, he didn't want anything to do with his brother's handouts, even in the form of beautiful Isobel Buckley.

"Oh, now, stop that fidgeting and take it like a man. I know you can handle it."

She paused long enough to make him fidget again. "Anyway, I picked everything out myself."

"Everything?" he asked warily.

"Every last piece."

He gazed at her warily. "Piece of what?

Dutch apple pie, I hope."

She chuckled. "You wish. You men and your stomachs. I'm sorry to disappoint you, but I'm speaking of clothes, as I think you already know."

He cringed again. "I was hoping you wouldn't say that. And yet, somehow I knew deep down in my heart, despite my growling stomach, that was what you were going to say. I wonder why?"

She propped her hands on her hips, and he knew she wasn't buying his propaganda. "If I didn't know better I'd think you were afraid of new clothes."

He chuckled, placing a fist on his hip, mimicking her moves and her voice. "If I didn't know you better, I'd think you were obsessed by them."

She tossed him a catty grin. "What an astute observation. How long did it take you to come up with that one?"

They stared at each other. A silent moment passed between them.

"So?" Dustin asked, amused, though maybe still a little uncomfortable. He was not in a big hurry to get to the *clothes* part, but resigned himself to the inevitable.

"So?" Isobel repeated, obviously pulling back from her thoughts and looking a little dazed.

"So are you going to get those new clothes out of your car so I can see them, or what?"

"I . . . uh . . ." Isobel stammered. "I wasn't thinking about the clothes," she admitted, her words muddled together as they tumbled from her mouth.

Dustin threw both hands up to his unshaven cheeks and drew in a sharp, dramatic breath. "You've astonished me."

She narrowed her eyes on him.

"It's a compliment." He nodded his head vigorously when she raised her eyebrow.

"Hmm . . . I wonder."

"Well," he prompted with a grin, "if you weren't thinking about what an incredibly changed man I'll be in your new clothes, just what exactly were you thinking about?"

She cleared her throat and looked out the window. "Your music," she mumbled under her breath.

"My what?"

"The piano. I followed the sound into your house. Although in my defense I did try knocking on the front door first."

Her face was a delightful shade of pink, growing red, and Dustin's grin widened.

"And of course I didn't hear you. I pound around so voraciously on these old ivories it makes the dogs howl clear down the street."

She lifted an eyebrow.

"And just wait until I start wailing along with the music," he added, laughing with her. "I'll have the whole neighborhood up in arms in a matter of minutes."

"I'm sure that isn't true," she replied instantly. "From what I heard of your piano playing, you're pretty good." She paused. "Actually, that's an understatement. If you sing half as well as you play, you'll have no trouble impressing me."

"Is that what I'm doing?" he queried lightly, his gaze brushing over her.

She swallowed hard and straightened her hair with her palm. "You tell me."

Not in a million years, he thought as his heart raced as fast as his thoughts. He wasn't about to admit to anything but his name, rank and serial number. And that was if he could speak at all.

He ran his fingers across the ivories, so swiftly that they didn't make a sound. It was one of the nicest feelings in the world, his fingers on the keyboard.

"I do love playing," he admitted softly.

"Play something now, then. For me?" Her voice was soft and so compelling he didn't even think about toying with her.

With a clipped nod and pinched lips holding back any expression of emotion that might betray him, he brought both hands to the keyboard, brushed his fingers lightly across the ivories and began playing a familiar hymn. It was slow and emotional, and Dustin closed his eyes to capture every nuance.

Isobel also closed her eyes, savoring the beauty of one of her most beloved hymns. How had he known "The Old Rugged Cross" was one of her particular favorites?

Suddenly, Dustin switched gears and started playing an upbeat praise song Isobel recognized from one of the CDs in her car. He was hitting so many notes one after the other Isobel was certain his fingers must be flying over the keys.

Her eyes popped open in surprise and Dustin smiled at her without missing a beat.

"Sing with me," he said, and looked out toward the sunshine-jammed window before breaking into an upbeat tune with his deep baritone.

"Oh, no, I don't think —"

"Isobel." Dustin cut her off with a warning look. "Remember, I know how to be every bit as stubborn as you do."

"Yes, but I —"

"Is-o-bel." He drew out her name, pleading this time instead of ordering.

She couldn't resist the soulful look he gave her with his big green eyes. For some reason this appeared to be very important to him, and she immediately capitulated to his endearing puppy-dog look.

"Okay, but don't say I didn't warn you," she said with a laugh.

"I will take full responsibility for your actions," he assured her, joining her laughter as their gazes met and held.

"Now, let's see," he said, flipping through a stack of books on the top of the piano. "What do you think we should sing?"

" 'Mary Had a Little Lamb'?" Isobel suggested, placing a hand over her mouth to suppress the laughter surging from her.

"Come now, Belle," he said fondly. "Surely you can do better than that!"

"You choose, then," Isobel said, suddenly tense. She was not at all comfortable with her own voice, though she hesitated to mention her fears to Dustin. "Just make it something easy."

Once again massaging the keys with his fingers before he started playing, Dustin broke into a simple praise melody Isobel was completely familiar with, one with a straightforward melody and without much range.

It figured.

He couldn't choose a song she'd never heard before, so she could honestly beg off.

It had to be the most likely song in the world she *might* be able to sing.

Oh, well. It was his problem. He'd asked for it, and had more or less told her to sing.

He might just come to rue it.

She joined in, tentatively at first and then, as Dustin smiled his encouragement, slowly and steadily with more gusto.

She couldn't have been more surprised if he had pinched her.

It was *fun* singing with Dustin.

Her voice might not be anything to write home about, but his certainly was, and for some odd reason she almost felt as if they sounded good together, as if their voices somehow blended.

But of course that was ridiculous. Water and oil didn't mix, no matter how hard a person might shake them.

She was relieved when the song ended.

Dustin sat straight-backed on his piano stool, staring at her, his hands folded in his lap.

When she finally had the nerve to look at him, he merely raised an eyebrow.

"What?" she finally asked when he continued to sit stone-faced and unspeaking.

"Well?" he prompted in return, looking and sounding as if he expected something from her.

"Well, what?" she asked, exasperated. She couldn't stand to play games, especially right now when she was feeling self-conscious. She was embarrassed enough as it was, without him rubbing it in.

"What was the big shock I was supposed to experience when you sang?" he asked her bluntly, looking her right in the eyes.

"What do you mean?"

He shrugged, as if the answer were obvious. "From the way you talked, I expected — well, I don't know — something awful."

"Wasn't it?" Shock rippled through her body at his intimation.

"No. Not at all." His voice was warm and reassuring.

"But I thought . . . my voice . . . I mean I really can't . . ." she stammered, but he cut her off with a shake of his head.

"What?" he asked, his voice gentle and firm. "You can't *what?*"

She didn't answer. She couldn't. She just stared at him, knowing he would force the issue anyway, but unable to say the word.

"Sing?" he suggested in a whisper, his gaze full of compassion.

She let out a relieved breath she hadn't realized she'd been holding. "Exactly."

Somehow, it was easier when he put it into words for her.

"Isobel, you have a nice voice. Trust me."

He sounded so genuine Isobel's heart did a flip-flop into her throat.

"I don't sing off-key?" she asked, her voice squeaking with surprise.

"Who told you that?" He sounded more surprised than she felt.

She blushed, trying to think where she'd first received that impression and what had led her to feel that way. "Why, no one, I guess. I used to sing all the time when I was a toddler and in preschool," she remembered with a sudden fondness. "I always liked music, especially Sunday school songs."

Her mind drifted to less happy times. "I remember," she said, choking on the words, "that my mother used to yell at me when I would sing."

"Aw, Belle," Dustin said, empathy dripping from every syllable. "Everyone's parents holler at their kids when they get too loud."

"Yes," Isobel replied quietly. "I know. I probably am making a big deal out of nothing." Her heart ached, screaming to the contrary.

In a moment he was by her side, grasping her hands gently in his, stroking her fingertips in a calm, rhythmic manner. "Of course, it's not nothing," he said in a gravelly tone.

He paused a moment and continued fervently, "Talk to me."

He led her to the couch and seated them both, never letting go of her hands.

"I remember a specific time," Isobel said slowly, looking over his shoulder so she wouldn't have to meet his eyes.

He nodded. "Go on."

"I was about five, I think. My mother was on the phone. I was singing with the television — one of those old children's programs. I didn't know who Mom was talking to, or that it was important. But suddenly she slammed the phone down and turned on me. Her face was as white as paper, and I remember noticing how bad she was shaking."

Dustin continued stroking her fingers with light reassurance.

"She yelled and yelled, until her face was bright red. She said my voice was annoying, and she wished for once I would just shut up. She kept yelling the words 'shut up' over and over again."

"She was in a really bad way," Dustin said. "Did you ever find out what was going on?"

Isobel shook her head. "I never did find out what that phone call was about. I always thought it must have been my father, but I don't know. I do know I never sang again."

"So you assumed that you must sing off-key?" he asked seriously.

She could feel her face growing warmer by the moment. "I don't know. I thought perhaps I was tone deaf. I always stand quietly in church and let others do the singing, though I praise God in my heart."

"You should sing," he admonished promptly, wagging a finger at her.

She shrugged, asking with her gaze for him to tell her what he was thinking.

"In the first place, Belle, today you hit every single note right on key, with a beautiful tone of voice I'm sure many people would love to hear."

"Oh," she said mildly.

"And second of all, you broke through today, Isobel. You sang with me. Don't go backward from here.

"Third," he said, his voice turning a little gruff, "that's not the point of music in the first place."

"I'm not following you," she said, honestly confused by his words.

"What is music really for, Isobel?" he queried seriously. He stood and returned to his piano stool, leaning his elbows on his knees and staring right into her eyes.

When she was silent, he answered his own

question. "To worship God."

"Of course," she whispered reverently. It was something she'd always known, yet Dustin was showing it to her in a new way.

"And do you think God cares if a person sings a bit off-key? If he sings from the heart, I expect that song comes off as beautiful to God's ears as the entire heavenly host put together."

Isobel just stared at him.

His smile wavered and he pinched his lips together. "And I'm preaching, aren't I?"

She shook her head. "No. Not at all. I've never heard it put that way. You're absolutely right. And it's a lovely thought."

She looked away from his bright gaze, seeking refuge in one of the posters lining his walls.

"What?" he asked.

She laughed at herself for her own folly. "I'm somewhat hesitant to admit this, but I wasn't thinking of God's ears so much as yours."

Dustin broke into laughter.

She was cute, that one. Cute, truly intelligent and completely fun to be around. He loved the way she spoke her mind no matter what, even if it got her into trouble or was potentially embarrassing.

He could respect a woman like that.

But that was more than he wanted her to know. He felt vulnerable enough around her as it was.

In fact, he couldn't ever remember a time in his life when a woman had touched his soul as she had in three short weeks. She was truly unique, and he silently thanked God for the opportunity to get to know her better.

What had started as an unmitigated disaster of a plan concocted by his brother was now time Dustin found himself looking forward to, more and more as the days went by.

He only had three weeks left.

Chapter Ten

Isobel was still staring at him, a peculiar look on her face, when Dustin started from his reverie and realized he'd been woolgathering.

"Why did you stop singing completely? After a while, didn't you wonder?"

"Well I never . . . I mean, other people were so . . . and I . . ." She paused from her stammering and took a deep breath. "You can't really know if you're good or not," she finished lamely. "After a while, it just seemed easier that way. Besides, my voice sounds different to my ears than it does everyone else's."

He decided to interrupt her soliloquy and spare her further agony.

"Isobel, sweetheart, let me put you out of your misery. You have a sweet, pleasant alto and you hit every note right on key."

"No squeaking?"

"Nothing remotely reminiscent of any

kind of animal," he assured her, shaking his head and chuckling at his own joke.

"Oh," she said, still sounding surprised and a little stunned. "Thank you."

"And remember, I'm a musician, so I know what I'm talking about."

"You are that," she agreed readily. "Who was your teacher? Where in the world did you learn to play the piano like that?"

It was an obvious attempt to change the subject, but Dustin let it go.

He coughed and brushed his fingers across the ivories, trying unsuccessfully to hide a bittersweet smile. "I didn't."

"You didn't what?"

"Have lessons," he admitted painfully. "Although in my defense, I did practice several hours every day when I was a kid."

"No one taught you," she repeated, sounding stunned.

He could tell she didn't believe him.

"My parents didn't believe in the extracurricular — except maybe for competitive sports, and that was my brother's department, not mine. Anything in the arts was definitely out of the question."

"But your dad was a multimillionaire!" she exclaimed. "Surely he could afford something as simple as piano lessons."

Dustin ground his teeth against the first

reaction that stabbed through his chest and threatened to exit his mouth. He would not say aloud how much it hurt him, no matter how soulfully her eyes looked at him and begged for him to share.

It took him a good moment to regain his composure, and the fact that Isobel was scowling — presumably on his behalf at his mistreatment by his parents — made the task of pulling himself together even more arduous.

It would be easier if he didn't know she cared. But for some reason, she did. It showed in her glistening brown eyes and in her hurt expression.

"My father was a strict businessman," Dustin explained hoarsely. "He worked his way up from a poor family to a multimillionaire by sheer effort and willpower. Frankly, he didn't see the point of studying fine arts, so we didn't."

"But there was a piano in your home," she said, stating the obvious.

"Oh, yes," he said, drowning out her last word. He had lived in a house, but despite his mother's best efforts, he realized now it had never really been *home* to him.

He squeezed his eyes shut and cleared his throat again. This was more difficult than he would ever have imagined. "It was the most expensive grand piano they could find. It was purely for aesthetic purposes, to make the room nice. It didn't mean anything significant to anyone. No one ever played it."

"Except you."

"Except me." He felt hollow inside as he made the admission, yet he felt compelled to go on, to tell her the whole story before he lost his nerve.

"My father was almost always away from home, building his business, so I rarely saw him. Every time my mother left the house to shop or meet with her friends, I practiced on the piano."

Isobel's eyes were bright with unshed tears, as she moved to stand behind Dustin, and he swallowed hard.

"That must have been hard for you," she whispered, placing her small, soft hand on his arm.

He nodded. "It was. I didn't have any music books or anything to work with at first. I had to wing it completely on my own."

"You succeeded admirably."

He nodded to acknowledge her compliment, and then continued with his story, his voice coarse with emotion. "When my mother died, music was my only solace. I bought music books and put what I learned on my own to use, learning notes and staffs and keys and stuff."

"All on your own?" she asked softly. "Without any help from anyone?"

"Not a soul even knew I played the piano until long after I'd reached adulthood."

"I can't believe your father," Isobel said angrily, squeezing his arm in protest. "I'm surprised you aren't permanently emotionally scarred by what that man did — or rather, didn't do."

"Who says I'm not?" he joked, forcing a chuckle through his dry throat.

"Dustin," she retorted, moving to sit on the soft leather sofa opposite the piano. Leaning forward, she ran her fingers casually over the coffee table, as if examining its planes and ridges.

"Play me a song," she urged him. "Something sweet and classical."

"Whatever the lady wants," he said with a wink, glad to have something positive to do, something to take the sad expression from Isobel's face.

He ran his fingers across the keys as was his unconscious habit, and then was instantly lost in the beautiful music of Bach. It happened all at once, as it had in childhood, his forgetting all his problems and cares as music swept him away.

He closed his eyes, savoring every note and measure, wanting the music to be especially pleasing to Isobel's ear.

He wanted her to hear what he heard, feel what he felt with music.

As he finished the piece, he took a deep, cleansing breath and turned to see how Isobel liked it, hoping the music had brought some manner of peace to her, as it had done with him.

To his surprise, she didn't appear to have been listening at all.

But when she turned to him, her eyes were glowing. "Bach was wonderful, and despite what it may look like, I really was listening to you."

"Glad to hear it. It sure didn't look to me like you were listening," he groused under his breath, trying not to look like a pouting child.

"All I can say is that you continue to impress and astound me. Your piano, your singing, your work at the flower shop — you are truly gifted by God in so many ways."

"Hobbies," he corrected. "Believe me, I'm no kind of genius or anything."

"You know, I don't think I even *have* a hobby. I spend all my time working. At night I get takeout and then fall into bed completely exhausted."

Dustin laughed, genuinely this time. "That's not good for you, you know."

"I know, I know. It's a bad habit of mine that I just can't seem to break."

Isobel was suddenly aware that she had intruded on his privacy. She had quite literally walked in on him when she hadn't even been invited into his house. And then she had continued to push and prod him around his house as if she owned it.

"I'm sorry," she blurted, feeling her face flush with heat. "I came here to give you clothes, not to take up your whole day with my prattling. Let me go get them for you."

She rushed out of the room and out of the house, gulping fresh air as she exited the door, and feeling just a little bit faint.

What was it about Dustin that made her long to linger? She would have to watch herself around him. She seemed to lose brain cells when he was near.

She pulled out a folding clothing rack and set it up with one hand, a trick she'd learned in college. She then carefully placed each outfit on it in what she would consider a reasonable order.

She smiled as she surveyed the colorful variety of materials and fabrics. Dustin would definitely be overwhelmed by the quantity and magnitude of her gift. She'd have to try to go easy on him so he didn't have a heart attack on her.

Carefully, she wheeled the rack up the driveway and bounced it up the single cement step to the porch, using both hands to stabilize the shaky rack.

Dustin came to help her, propping open the screen door for her, opening the main door wide, then holding the screen with one foot so he could assist her as they yanked and pulled till they had the rack in the carpeted foyer.

It was frustrating but not impossible to trek toward the den on the thick plush carpet, with both of them working at it. The wheels squeaked and groaned, complaining all the way.

Isobel sighed in relief when she reached the den. "That was quite a challenge," she said. "I have a tuxedo for you for the Elway benefit," she teased. "It's black, with a black-and-white-striped ascot. You'll look great in it."

When he didn't reply, Isobel thought he was being stubborn. She turned, expecting to see Dustin by her side, frowning and throwing a boyish, if adorable, fit.

"Thanks for coming today," Dustin said gruffly, not looking at her.

"I was glad to. I — I'm glad you weren't angry with me for intruding."

"Never," he said, opening his arms to her. Isobel stepped into his embrace without a word. With her head resting against his chest where she could hear the rapid beat of his heart, there seemed to be nothing left to say.

CHAPTER ELEVEN

Dustin was in his flower shop completing an arrangement for a wedding, but his heart wasn't really in it. Try as he might, he just couldn't keep his mind on his work.

He had discovered a soft side to Isobel, a woman he'd first thought was made of steel and who might not possess a heart at all.

Shows how much he knew.

She was a woman who followed classical music to its source without considering the consequences.

This Isobel followed her heart before her head. She was willing to take a chance even when she thought she'd fail, like singing when she thought she couldn't carry a tune.

He laughed at that now. How sweet she was, tentatively singing the praise song despite her fear, not realizing that not only was she right on key, but that she had a sweet, pleasing voice.

Why hadn't anyone ever told her what a

lovely singing voice she had? Of course, if she never sang, that would pretty much explain it.

Well, he decided, jamming flowers into the arrangement with both fists, *he* was going to tell her. And he'd tell her over and over again until she believed him.

Until she believed in herself.

Suddenly, he knew what he had to do, and it couldn't wait, not one more second. He stopped arranging the bouquet and told the two employees hard at work he was leaving.

He couldn't remember being this excited about anything in a long, long time.

Maybe ever.

Making one quick stop at a local music store, he hurried home, anxious to begin this new project he'd concocted on a whim but knew in his heart might be one of the best ideas he'd ever had.

Once home, he shed his coat and went straight to the piano. With gentle reverence, he opened his new package and carefully placed the lined, blank staff sheets before him.

For a moment he felt overwhelmed, about to dive in far over his head with nothing but one quick gulp of air. The lines and blank spaces were intimidating, challenging him to fill in the notes.

Could he really do this?

He'd never composed music before, only played it. He hadn't the remotest notion of whether he could create a piece of his own, compose his own melody and write his own words.

Yet he had to try.

For her.

Besides, to his surprise, music was already beginning to form in his head. He realized it was already there, fully formed in his mind. All *he* had to do was get it down on paper.

Soon he was completely involved in the project, a pencil behind his ear and that stubborn lock of hair falling down on his forehead.

It was more complicated than he thought it would be, but he was certainly improving as he went along.

He was writing music!

He realized now it would take quite some time to finish the piece, far longer than he'd originally thought. But he was determined to complete it before the six weeks were up, so he could give a gift back to Belle for all she'd done for him.

Dustin didn't raise his head for several hours. He was so fascinated by the process of putting the music in his head onto paper that he threw himself wholeheartedly into the work.

When he looked at the clock, it was ten after seven at night. At first he thought he might go back and work some more, but there was something else niggling at his brain, something he was supposed to remember.

What was it?

He was growling under his breath about how he needed to start writing things down so he could remember his appointments, when it hit him.

He was supposed to be at the John Elway Foundation benefit. It was a high-class event and Dustin knew Isobel had had to pull strings and call in some favors to get invited.

And, he realized with a sharp spike in his adrenaline, he was supposed to be there at seven o'clock sharp.

He was late.

Really late, since he still had to put on the tuxedo Isobel had left him. And then it was at least a thirty-minute drive downtown, and that was if the traffic was good.

He looked in the mirror, critically surveying his appearance. His hair was a bit mussed, but that could be easily remedied with a comb and some gel. His black T-shirt was brand-new, and his jeans were still discernibly black, through a bit faded in spots.

He shuffled though the clothes rack Isobel had brought him and immediately came upon a nice black-and-gray sports coat. He chuckled and pulled it down from the rack even as his plan formed.

Isobel would have to be pleased by his ingenuity in the heat of tardiness.

Besides, he didn't like tuxedos anyway.

Isobel stood in the corner of the large, highly decorated conference room and watched the entrance door like a hawk. Occasionally she would tap her foot in an impatient rhythm.

Where in the world was Dustin?

He'd *promised* to be her escort tonight, and though she was generally quite comfortable mingling with the crowds on her own in such situations, for some reason tonight she felt as if a part of her was missing.

It was an unsettling notion, and Isobel didn't really like it. Certainly she wouldn't mention her awkward feelings to anyone, especially Dustin.

If he showed up.

She would not look at her watch again, knowing it would only be one or two minutes since the last time she'd looked.

Instead, she looked again at the door, thinking he might be planning to make a grand entrance just to surprise her and throw her off guard, as Dustin was so very fond of doing.

For a moment she dwelled on that unlikely fantasy, most especially the first glance of Dustin in a tuxedo. She had no doubt he would be breathtakingly gorgeous. Tuxedos always made men look dashing and elegant, but she suspected Dustin would look especially charming.

But he wasn't there.

At least she thought he wasn't until she made a casual sweep of the room and her gaze stopped on Dustin. He was at the opposite end of the crowd, already in an animated conversation with the mayor of Denver.

No wonder she hadn't recognized him. She'd been looking for a man in black.

What was he wearing?

Though he was obviously unaware of it, Dustin looked as if he'd crawled out from under a rock, and Isobel wanted nothing more at that moment than to crawl right underneath the very rock Dustin had come out of — after she'd had a chance to wring his neck.

Steam rose from the tips of her toes to the tops of her ears.

He had *promised!*

On time, and dressed in a tuxedo.

Zero for two, by her count.

How could he do this to her?

As if sensing her stare, Dustin turned around and looked straight at her. His smile brightened noticeably as he saluted her with his hand. He then turned to the mayor, said something that made the mayor chuckle and made a beeline for Isobel.

"Hey, Belle, I've been talking to the mayor. Did you know he goes to —"

"You're late," she said flatly, cutting him off. She was in no mood for his cheerful chatter. She had so many things she wanted to say to him that her words were all mixed up in her head. "You — you —"

"Wrascally Wrabbit?" he suggested, chuckling at his own jest.

"How can you joke at a time like this?" she demanded in a huff of hot air.

He made a sweeping gesture that encompassed the whole room. "Is this a party, or what?" he asked in a bright voice, obviously ignoring the female warning signs she was inwardly wrestling with and which she was sure showed in her posture and on her face, not to mention in her voice.

"Yes, Dustin. It's a party. An *upscale* party," she emphasized.

He merely shrugged.

"Look how everyone is dressed — in tuxedos and cocktail dresses. This was supposed to be a test drive of the new you, remember? All I see is the same old Dustin Fairfax."

He looked down at his own clothing and frowned. "Well, yes," he admitted with a groan. "I had noticed I'm a bit underdressed, but then, I usually am."

"And your excuse is?"

He looked at her blankly for a moment. "My excuse," he repeated halfheartedly. "Am I supposed to have an explanation?"

He looked a bit rattled by the simple request, which surprised Isobel for a moment. She'd expected him to be blurting wild excuses a mile a minute.

But he wasn't.

Isobel took that moment to push him.

"I'm sure it's fascinating, how you were on your way to the benefit and some homeless person needed to borrow your tuxedo for a night out on the town."

"Hey," he protested. "Lay off, already. I have a good reason."

"I'm sure you do," she said wryly. "I'm just surprised you haven't divulged it yet.

You always seem to surprise me."

"I . . . it's just that I was . . ." His eyes lit up even as he struggled for words.

He stopped suddenly, set his jaw and met her eyes squarely. "I was busy with a project at the house, and I lost track of time. It's as simple as that."

"And the clothes?" she prompted.

"I thought you would want me to be here as soon as possible, so I improvised and rushed to get here as quickly as I could. I've been to these events before, Belle. I knew the choice I was making."

His excuse sounded lame to both of them, but Isobel found her heart softening to him. Why did he always have that effect on her?

"Did I mention I'm more comfortable than any other man here?"

She glared at him.

"Please, Isobel," he begged softly. He touched her arm and implored her with his soft green eyes.

Suddenly he was serious, his tone grave. "*Please* don't ask me to explain more than I have. I can't." He frowned. "I won't. Can you find it in your heart to forgive me?"

She couldn't help it. Her heart capitulated.

She reached up and touched the hard line of his chin, running her finger along the rough-whiskered edge. "You missed a spot."

"Did I?" he asked, chuckling. "Guess that's what happens when you try to shave and tie your sneakers at the same time."

Her eyes dropped to his well-worn sneakers, her gaze once again full of surprise.

Dustin inwardly cringed. As soon as he had said the words, he realized he had just brought the subject back to his clothes, which was the last thing he wanted to talk about and certainly the very last thing he wanted Isobel to be thinking about.

Holding his breath and expecting a firm reprimand, he was saved by the announcement of dinner being served.

He breathed a sigh of relief as people immediately began milling around them, looking for their place cards among the many tables and making far too much noise for anyone to have a real conversation.

"Where are we?" he asked, moving closer to her. After a moment, he placed an arm around her shoulders to keep them from being separated by the hungry crowd.

She reached into her bag and drew out a carefully folded piece of paper. "Table eight," she said, glancing across the room. "Although I admit I'm not sure where that is. I should have checked earlier."

He slid his hand down across her waist

and then slid his hand into hers, linking her fingers with his. Isobel suddenly forgot what she was doing as the pad of his thumb stroked over hers.

She shook her head in confusion.

"Don't worry. I know where it is," he said, winking down at her and squeezing her hand. "I saw it when I came in. Just stick with me."

Dustin was glad he had taken the time to look, so this time, anyway, he could come off as the hero.

Gallantly offering his arm, he escorted her to the table and held a chair for her. She was glowing with pleasure, and he suddenly realized that she was completely in her element here — the fine dining, fancy clothes and fancy talk.

He, on the other hand, felt completely overwhelmed. Too many people, too much noise and definitely too much silverware.

It wasn't that he'd never seen such a layout, but he hadn't used one since he was a kid under the instruction of his nanny and the cook before a big dinner at their home. And even then he'd been relegated to the kids table with only one fork and no knife at all.

"I — er —" He paused and cleared his throat. Leaning in close to her ear, he whispered, "Why doesn't everyone just use one fork and scrap the rest of the silver? Less for the dishwashing folks, you know?"

She chuckled and tapped his nose playfully with her finger. "You can be really adorable sometimes, do you know that?"

Her words created a funny, fluttering feeling in his gut. He cocked an eyebrow and flashed her a cheeky smile. "I hope so."

Using her index finger under his chin to pull him closer to her, she whispered, "The small, sharp fork is for appetizers. Next to that is the one for salad. Then you have your main-dish fork."

He turned his head just slightly, putting them eye-to-eye and nearly touching foreheads. "Whose idea was it to make it so complicated?" he asked in a stage whisper that he knew didn't mask his alarm. "My father's, probably."

"Let's keep it simple," she said with a small nod that closed the gap between their foreheads until they were touching. Her brown eyes beamed with fondness and amusement. "There's a trick to it. Start on the outside and work in."

"Perfect," he said, his voice softening even as his gaze warmed on the beautiful woman beside him. "And I mean you, not the silverware. Although now that you mention it, I do recall Nanny saying something to that effect."

Without conscious thought, he leaned in slowly, crossing the small gap between his lips and hers.

His heart racing in his chest, he gave her plenty of time to figure out what he was doing, to be the one who, in the end, made the choice.

Though her arm stiffened under his hand, she didn't move a muscle to pull away from him. Only her eyes, her breathlessly warm brown eyes that felt as if they were staring right into his soul, widened slightly.

He didn't need more confirmation than that. He took her gaze as a yes and closed his eyes as he brushed his lips over the bee-stung softness of hers.

At the touch of his lips on hers, Isobel slammed back in her chair so intensely she thought she might tip herself over. She quickly tucked her elbows into her side to keep from flapping around in what she supposed would be a most inelegant manner.

If she fell, she fell; but she wouldn't make a scene doing so.

Dustin, too, pulled back, but his movement was only to straighten his spine and turn his gaze straight forward, away from her. He looked every bit as stunned as she felt, as if he hadn't initiated the contact.

"Sorry," he said gruffly. "I forgot you work for my brother."

Isobel felt the impact of his words like a dart in her heart. She hadn't meant to have it look as if she were turning *away* from his kiss — it was the sweetest moment she had ever known.

In that moment, she had finally come to the realization that Dustin wasn't just some sort of challenging makeover project.

And she was attracted to that man, as a woman was drawn to a man. He was no longer a challenging project.

He was a man.

But that wasn't the reason she had jerked away. It was a sudden sense of guilt that had caused the fatal movement.

He was her client — at least in a sense. And although there were no set doctor/patient types of rules in the fashion industry, she was struck by her own sense of responsibility to the work she'd been hired to do, and to those she was accountable to.

It was a silly thing, really. She considered herself rational and down-to-earth, and here she was being flighty and nonsensical.

She attempted to smile at him, but he would have none of it. He was pretending she wasn't even there. She had never seen

Dustin look so grim, not even when faced with a table full of silverware.

He was punching into his salad — with the correct fork — as if he had to spear and kill the lettuce in order to eat it.

And he wouldn't look at her, or even in her direction. Not for one second.

He was polite and cheerful with the other guests at the table, keeping the conversation moving right along, but Isobel could tell something was wrong and she knew she was the cause of it.

Oh, why had she pulled away from him? He was taking it all wrong.

Try as she might, she could not engage Dustin's attention. Throughout the meal, she attempted to add to the conversation, especially when Dustin was voicing his own opinions.

But he wouldn't speak to her, wouldn't even look at her.

Not a glance.

It appeared the only way she was *really* contributing to the evening was in making the most easygoing, laid-back man she had ever known become stiff and tense.

Frustrated, she got up and began milling around the room, unsuccessfully attempting to put Dustin and his ill humor out of her mind.

As if that were possible.

What was she supposed to do?

Apologize?

Ask for another kiss so she could do it right and not offend him this time?

In the end, she decided it would have to be his move. She'd just have to wait and see.

CHAPTER TWELVE

Isobel waited.

She waited. And waited. And waited.

For a whole week she waited.

By the following Saturday, she had decided Dustin wasn't planning to contact her at all.

Ever.

Why she should be surprised by that was beyond her, she decided. After all, she was the one hired to make over Dustin, and not the other way around. She should be contacting him.

Not to mention the fact she was certain she had offended him when she'd pulled away from his kiss at the charity banquet.

No wonder he wasn't calling her. Who wanted to be rejected?

She should have followed up the next day, she realized, mentally kicking herself for her tactical error. She'd been acting as if she were in an emotional relationship with

Dustin, not as his image consultant, which was the truth of the matter.

He owed her nothing.

She owed him a job well done.

What had she been thinking?

She could have — *should have* — called him Sunday afternoon and professionally reviewed what he *should* have worn to the banquet. She should have been calm, cool, collected and proficient.

The truth was that he had pulled it off. And in all honesty, it hadn't bothered her as much as it should have, especially given her profession.

Maybe it was just that the look was completely, uniquely Dustin.

Of course, critiquing his clothing would no doubt have led to an argument, but at the very least they would have been talking. And they'd always worked out their differences before.

Now, too much time had passed for her to call and nag him about his clothing selections. In fact, try as she might, she couldn't think of one single viable reason to call him now at all.

Short of the money — and she refused to be that shallow ever again.

She had dropped the ball.

She was still mulling over her dilemma

when the phone rang, intruding on her thoughts like rapid gunfire. She jumped and put a hand to her chest to still her banging heart.

"Isobel?"

"Dustin!" she exclaimed. She hoped she didn't sound as relieved as she felt, but knew he could probably hear the excitement in her voice. "It's good to hear from you."

"Yeah," he said with a chuckle. She could imagine him shaking his head in mirth. "I kind of thought you would call me on Sunday and chew me out for my jeans and T-shirt combination."

She laughed, relieved at his usual warmth and candor. "Your jeans, your T-shirt and a few other choice items." His tennis shoes came to mind.

"Why didn't you?" he asked, sounding suddenly serious, his voice low and gruff. "Call me, I mean. Surely my tennis shoes alone are worth a few good words, if nothing else. I was really surprised when you didn't contact me at all. Not even a phone call."

"I . . ." Isobel started, and then stopped again. She was about to say she had been afraid to make contact with him after the way she had acted, which was the truth of the matter.

But she couldn't tell the truth. She felt vulnerable enough simply thinking the thoughts. To dare to speak them aloud was unimaginable.

"I was busy," she said, amazed at how calm and sure her voice sounded to her own ears. She didn't sound shaky at all.

She wasn't accustomed to lying, and as she said the words the remorse she felt in her heart made itself into a prayer for God's ears. Later, she would have to apologize to Dustin.

"Busy?" Dustin repeated, laughing loudly. It sounded forced to Isobel's ears. Guilt gushed over her like an ice-cold waterfall.

"Too busy for me? But I'm supposed to be first on your schedule," he complained, his lips tight. "I'm sure my brother made that clear to you, and I'm pretty sure he's paying you a load of cash to see that I'm first on your *busy* agenda."

"Why, yes," she said, not able to hide her surprise at his vehemence. He sounded almost as if he were chastising her, like a parent with a child, and her hackles rose. "You *are* my highest priority, of course. I had a matter which I could not put off. It was — unavoidable."

"I see," Dustin's voice softened though he still sounded strongly suspicious.

She knew he didn't believe her, yet his next words were, "I'm not going to press you, Isobel."

Her throat tightened until she felt she was choking. She couldn't have spoken if she'd been given a million dollars to do so.

How did he understand her so well when she didn't even understand herself?

"Well then, Belle," Dustin said, his pure baritone caressing each syllable. "Can you come out with me *today?*"

"Yes, but, wh-where are we going?" she stammered, suddenly unable to keep her nervousness in check any longer.

Dustin could hear the hesitance in her voice. "Did you already have other plans made? Because we can always postpone if you'd rather. It does have a direct correlation with fashion, however."

He really wanted to spend the day with her, but couldn't help himself in giving her an out if she didn't want to go.

"Then how could I possibly refuse?" she immediately reassured him, though Dustin thought her tone was rather forced and affected.

Dustin restrained a laugh. "Perfect. I'll pick you up in a half hour. That is, if you tell me how to get to your house."

"It's a condo," she corrected halfheartedly. "I'll give you directions. But where are we going? I don't recall you saying."

"I didn't say," he replied cheerfully. "It's a surprise."

"Surprise?" she repeated, her interest clearly piqued, judging by the high, squeaky tone to her voice.

He laughed with his whole heart. What woman didn't like surprises?

A little more than a half hour later, Dustin arrived at Isobel's house. The moment he rang the doorbell, she opened her front door. He wondered if she'd been waiting for him. She was dressed in a pretty pink number and even had a sweater tucked around her shoulders.

"Shall we go?" he asked, cordially offering his arm. She tucked her hand through the crook and smiled.

"Lead on, good gentleman."

He was happy to do so, and she was a willing participant, at least until she spied his means of transportation.

She stopped and stood as stiff as a brick wall, staring with her mouth pinched tightly shut and her eyes wide. Her hands were clenched into fists at her side.

He just grinned, having known this particular idea was going to take some selling on his part. "I take it you've never ridden on a motorcycle before."

She continued staring for a moment. "You could safely say that."

He struggled not to continue laughing, knowing Isobel would not appreciate his good humor. "Then this will be an adventure."

"Or a nightmare," she countered.

He surveyed her outfit again, a short skirt and a blouse made of some soft, silky pink material. And high heels.

"Go back in and change," he ordered lightly. "Jeans and a T-shirt. I won't take no for an answer, so you may as well just go."

"You're kidding, right?" Her expression clearly let him know she hoped he was jesting with her, and would pull a comfortable Towncar out of his pocket.

"Didn't I say this was a fashion expedition?" he prodded cheerfully, flashing her a cheeky grin.

She planted her hands on her hips and glared at him. "A T-shirt?"

"And tennis shoes," he continued as if she hadn't spoken at all. "You just can't ride a motorcycle in heels, Isobel, no matter how much you'd like to."

"But I —"

"Go!" He cut her off in a brisk, no-nonsense tone, chuckling as she dashed back up the walk.

Isobel appeared five minutes later in navy blue designer jeans, a red T-shirt that read Shopping Is my Therapy and a worn pair of white tennis shoes.

"Wow," Dustin said, whistling softly and running his hand along his jaw.

"Wow, what?" she said, flashing her gaze at him. "Are you making fun of me?"

His amused gaze met hers. "Well, to tell you the truth, Belle, I really didn't think you *owned* a pair of tennis shoes. And those even look well-used." He pointed to her feet. "I am impressed."

"Knock it off with the sarcasm, Dustin," she said, pushing his shoulder playfully. "I wear tennis shoes all the time."

He lifted his eyebrows in disbelief.

"I do," she said, pulling herself to her full height of five foot seven. "Inside my house. When I work *out.*"

He laughed heartily. "Today you're going to be wearing them out."

She hesitated. "I have a nice pair of black boots that —"

"Have a two-inch heel on them," Dustin finished for her.

She made a face at him.

"So I'm right."

"Don't gloat," she said, shaking her head

but smothering a laugh.

"Who's gloating?" he asked with a criminal grin. "I just like getting my way."

"I've noticed that."

This time he was the one to make the face. He then moved to his bike and removed the leather jacket and helmet he had stored at the rear of the seat and fastened down with bungee cords.

Isobel put the jacket on without comment, but when he held up the helmet, she threw her hands up and shrieked in earnest.

"Oh, must we?" she asked, shaking away from the helmet and putting both hands out in unconscious defense. "I have a lovely pair of sunglasses I can wear. That's the law, isn't it?"

Dustin rolled his eyes. "Isobel. Don't be stubborn. I don't give two hoots about the law. Your health might have crossed my mind, though."

"But my hair —"

"Will be all tangled and frizzy by the end of the ride with your sunglasses," Dustin cut in. "Unless, of course, you wear this."

He dangled the helmet in front of her by one finger.

"Helmet head," she muttered, but she took the offending headpiece and awkwardly placed it on her head nonetheless.

Grinning, Dustin adjusted the straps under her chin and made sure it was a secure fit.

"You'll live," he teased.

"That," she said with a pouting twist of the lips, "remains to be seen."

Isobel had never in her life even remotely considered riding on a motorcycle. The only risks she took were calculated.

She left the death-defying feats like motorbikes to men like Dustin.

So she was surprised at the pleasant surge of adrenaline that shot through her as she clutched her arms around Dustin's waist and he put the cycle in gear, quickly accelerating so the wind rushed around them and the cycle purred into life.

"Woo-hoo!" she shouted as they zipped through suburban back roads and Dustin showed off the capacity of his motorcycle.

"Fun, huh?" he yelled back at her.

"Can this thing go any faster?"

Dustin roared with laughter and cranked his bike up.

He never would have thought Isobel would actually *like* riding a motorcycle. He'd only brought it out to prove a point, and maybe because he was still a little angry at her shallow behavior at the benefit.

But all of that seemed inconsequential now.

It was a beautiful, sunshiny winter morning, so typical of Colorado weather and yet always an enjoyable surprise. He had a powerful vehicle beneath him, the wind whipping around him and a beautiful woman clutched to his back.

What more could a man ask for?

Impulsively, he popped a wheelie and buzzed down the street on one wheel. Isobel held him more tightly but seemed to make the move with grace.

She made some sort of sound he couldn't quite discern. He thought she might be laughing.

At the end of the street he pulled his bike to the side of the road and pulled his helmet off, scratching his fingers through his thick, ruffled black hair.

"How was that?" he asked, out of breath but with a smile on his face.

Isobel flipped her faceplate up. Her complexion was rosy and her brown eyes were sparkling with delight as she smiled back at him.

"Incredible," she answered, sounding out of breath. "I feel so . . ."

She hesitated at length, so he completed her sentence for her.

Several times.

"Free?" he suggested. "Alive? Impressed? All shook up?"

She laughed and waved her hand at him. "All of the above."

"You need some spontaneity in your life, Belle," he said sincerely. "Too much of your life is planned exactly by the book."

"Dustin," she said, pulling in a loud breath and placing her hand flat over her rapidly beating heart, "you are definitely all the spontaneity I can handle in one day."

He grinned widely.

"But no more pop-a-wheelies, okay? I thought I was going to slide right off the end of the motorbike. It's a good thing I had you to hold on to."

Now why did he not feel chagrined?

Instead, he threw back his head and laughed heartily. "Quite a jazz, isn't it?"

She nodded, the motion amplified by her oversized helmet. "It is that, yes." She paused, then poked him in the chest with her finger. "Don't do it again."

He laughed and grabbed her hand, giving it a gentle squeeze. "I promise. But we have to use the freeway to get where we're going today. Are you going to be okay with that?"

"Oh, sure," she agreed with a smile of anticipation that made her look childlike and vulnerable, and made Dustin's protective instinct surge to the surface. "Just no more —"

"Yeah, right," he agreed, knocking her helmet lightly with his fist. "I promise. No more pop-a-wheelies. At least for today."

Then he turned back in the seat and revved the motor, smiling to himself when she scooted in close to his back and clutched tightly to his waist.

CHAPTER THIRTEEN

Twenty minutes later he pulled up at their first stop of the day, a deep brown, stone-hewn church with stained glass windows and its front double doors painted a bright cherry-red, though the paint was peeling to show the wood beneath.

Isobel craned her neck up to see a pointed steeple complete with a belfry.

"A church?" she asked as she pulled her helmet off and brushed her hair back around her face. She didn't bother to state the obvious, that they weren't exactly in the best part of town.

Dustin swallowed hard. It was hard to concentrate on her words when the sunshine played off the highlights in her hair in such a beautiful way. "Where were you expecting to go?"

She placed her helmet on the cycle and fumbled with the bungee cords meant to tie it down. "I don't know. The only thing I can say for sure about you is that I can't say anything for sure about you."

"Hmm. And here I thought women were attracted to men of mystery," he said, swishing an imaginary cape across his shoulders.

Her face turned a delicate shade of pink and it took her a moment to answer. When she did, it was in a tight, squeaky voice. "I — uh — *they* do."

He opened his mouth to tease her some more, but she cut him off.

"In theory." She stared into his eyes. "But you know, in real life it can be — frustrating. Sometimes I feel like I don't know you at all."

"And sometimes I feel I know you better than anyone else on earth," he countered, crossing his arms over his chest.

They stared at each other for a long moment, each either unable or unwilling to break the tense moment by speaking.

Finally, Isobel broke eye contact and looked back up toward the steeple, gesturing at the big bell. "This is a really pretty church."

It was lame, but it was a start.

"Yeah," he agreed, his voice deep. "Too bad it's off the main way where no one can see it. Hardly anyone knows it's here."

He paused and ran his fingers through his

hair. "It's almost a hundred years old. But believe it or not, the bell still rings."

"How cool," she said. "But you still haven't told me why we are here."

"Tell you?" he asked with a wink. "How about I show you?"

He took her hand and pulled her toward the red doors. "I can't wait for you to see this."

With great aplomb, he opened one of the doors and gestured her in.

"I'm breathless with anticipation," she teased as she walked by him.

He yanked gently on the back of her silky dark hair as he followed up behind her.

"Belle," he whispered in her ear, causing a shiver to run all the way up her spine.

To Isobel's surprise, the small sanctuary was buzzing and alive with a veritable hive of teenagers. Though the room looked as if it would hold no more than twenty parishioners, there were at least forty youths hanging about.

From Isobel's perspective, they ranged from junior high to nearing high-school graduation. It was a beautiful sight, seeing all these kids together inside a church, with nearly every conceivable shade of skin represented — not to mention *hair* — and everyone smiling and mixing about.

But what was this about?

She turned to Dustin, questioning him about what she was seeing without saying a word.

"Watch and learn," he said with a clipped nod and a mysterious grin.

Nodding back at him, she slid into the last pew at the back of the sanctuary and leaned in to see what would happen.

As Dustin moved into the middle of activity, he experienced a moment of pure nerves that nearly made him freeze to the spot.

What would Isobel think about what was about to happen?

Would she understand the passion of his heart?

A moment later, he forgot to be nervous as the youths began gathering around him. He knew and loved each and every one of these kids.

"It's the music man," one of the older boys crowed loudly.

"Hey, Dugan," Dustin responded. The boy approached and they popped fists, then hands, and then wrapped their arms around each others' shoulders and gobbled like turkeys.

It was an old and traditional male sort of rite of passage, and Dustin didn't think anything of his usual decorum until he heard Isobel roaring with laughter in the background.

He turned to her and gave an elaborate mock bow before calling for the kids to get organized.

It took a few minutes and a lot of noise to get forty teenagers moving in the right direction, but eventually the kids were seated by section, and were relatively quiet and ready for his direction.

Moving to the piano, he said, "Let's start with some warm-ups, and then we'll go ahead and tackle the anthem for next Sunday."

As he ran scales for the teenagers to follow, he surreptitiously glanced back at Isobel to see how she was taking what was happening.

She was sitting straight-backed in the pew, her hands clasped in her lap and her face unreadable. Her gaze was glued to the teens, so he couldn't see her eyes to discern whether or not this meant something to her.

Well, maybe this would surprise her.

He ran his fingers over the ivories, as was his habit before playing, then cranked into a modern, upbeat version of "Amazing Grace."

The piece featured one girl soloist and one guy, who then came together in a touching duet in the middle of the last verse. The young voices had a purity to them he knew he would never find in adult voices, and he coveted every moment, feeling blessed to be their director.

He loved both the music and the words, and closed his eyes as the song ended, his heart reaching out to God in worship.

Praise God.

When he opened his eyes, his first act was to peer back at Isobel.

She had her eyes closed, too. He hoped that was a good thing.

The hour's practice flew by as Dustin led the choir in a variety of sacred tunes, some modern and some classic.

He was proud of his kids, proud to bursting. They had come far in the short time he had been teaching them, and not just vocally, either.

Spiritually, they had grown closer to each other and to God. Gone were the gang-type references and fist-fighting Dustin had dealt with in the beginning.

And as bad as the boys had been, the girls had been even worse, with their petty rivalries often blowing up into catfighting that easily put the boys' fistfights to shame.

Boys fought fair. Dustin knew what to expect from the male gender.

But girls?

Man, when their fur was flying, it was no holds barred. Girls used *all* their resources — scratching, pulling hair, biting, poking at eyes, using knees and elbows . . . Well, he was glad he'd worked past that stage with them for the most part.

Once again he glanced back at Isobel. She continued to sit straight-backed and unmoving, and her face gave nothing away.

Disappointment washed through Dustin.

He had trusted her, opened his heart to her and shown her a part of his life he'd kept secret from the world until now.

He thought she'd understand.

And she couldn't care less.

He set his jaw, gathered himself together and called for prayer time.

The kids gathered around, taking hands and speaking softly amongst themselves.

When he called for prayer requests, several of them jumped right in with their problems. One young lady's grandmother was in a hospital dying from cancer. A young man named Jay asked for prayer for his older brother, who he thought might be using drugs.

Suddenly he heard a soft, sweet voice behind him, as Isobel took his hand and joined the circle. A tingle spread down

Dustin's back.

"This isn't anywhere near as serious as some of the things I've heard from you," she said, making eye contact around the circle. "But I'd appreciate prayers for my mother. She's thinking of moving to Denver from a small town in Texas where she's lived all her life. It's a big move, and frightening."

She shrugged. "I guess she wants to be near her grandchildren. That is, if I ever get married. And if I ever have children."

The teens' reaction was half laughter, half hooting calls to Dustin to help out his girlfriend's mother and marry Isobel. They were especially interested in the *kids* part.

In response to their interest, Dustin couldn't help but give Isobel a smacking kiss on the cheek, which caused her to turn bright red, though she was laughing.

She flashed him a look that told him he had most definitely committed a major felony and ought to be ashamed of himself.

He absolutely wasn't feeling any sort of remorse, especially since he was enjoying the amusement of the teenagers immensely.

The kiss had been nice, too, though he'd never admit that to Isobel.

After the noise had died down to a bearable level, Dustin called for prayer.

The teens prayed openly and spontaneously for the needs that had been mentioned and some that hadn't. Isobel was squeezing his hand tightly, and he found himself rubbing the pad of his thumb against hers.

He wasn't sure why she was shaking with emotion until he peeked though one half-closed eye and saw there were tears on her face.

He wondered if *he* had somehow inadvertently made her cry, and then realized with a metaphorical thump in the head that he was thinking like a guy.

Isobel's tears were clearly tears of joy.

He closed his eyes, smiled and gripped her hand back tightly. Funny how the moment was suddenly causing a scratch in his own throat.

Probably just the start of a cold.

But whatever he told himself to explain away his own emotions, he couldn't deny the way his heart raced to life when he heard Isobel pray.

"Father, thank You for this blessed and talented group of youth, and for giving me the opportunity to enjoy their lovely voices today. These young people offer their voices as the purest form of worship, and their faith puts my own to shame. Shower them with Your love and blessing, Father, and I pray You'll address all their individual needs, both those spoken and those left unsaid."

The church was so quiet after Isobel's prayer that even the tiniest sound echoed. Dustin thought those around him must have been able to hear the frantic thump of his heart.

After a few more minutes, Dustin ended the prayer. "Thank You for hearing our needs, Father. All this we pray in Jesus' name. Amen."

The kids immediately broke into a buzz of activity, grabbing coats and purses and personal CD players. Many spoke to Isobel as they left, and her smile was genuine as she made compliment after compliment to each of the young people.

As the last of the youths left, the church once again became quiet. Dustin closed the red wooden doors and turned back, leaning against the old, solid wood. Isobel stood just where he'd left her, at the front of the sanctuary.

She had her arms clasped about herself as if she were feeling a chill, and her gaze arched up to the large cross at the front of the church.

"Thank you," she said quietly as he approached, her voice scratchy with emotion. "I know you risked a lot in bringing me here. Again, you've shown me a side of you that I *know* your brother doesn't know about, in allowing me to participate in what transpired today."

Participate. Not watch.

Dustin grinned. "They are a pretty awesome crew, aren't they?" he asked promptly. "I'm really proud of them."

"As you should be," she agreed in a heartbeat. "They are almost every bit as awesome as their wonderful director."

Before he could see it coming, she reached on tiptoe and kissed his cheek.

"Scratchy as usual," she complained in a teasing voice.

He ran a hand across his jaw, his mind still swimming. "Mmm. Yeah, uh, sorry."

"Don't be," she said, waving off the comment. "I find I'm getting used to the unshaved look. Who would have known?"

He laughed and ran a hand across her silky hair. "Should we call that progress?"

"Oh, no," she said, shaking her head. "I'm not the one on trial here. Besides, if anything, I'm moving backward."

He groaned. "Don't remind me."

"While we're on the subject . . ." Isobel began, and then stopped with a pregnant pause.

"Oh, what now?"

"This isn't about clothing," she assured him. "For now, anyway."

He blew out a breath and grinned at her. "That's a relief."

"However," she continued, automatically switching to her business voice as she faced him, "I do have a few questions."

"Shoot," he said, looking as if he meant it in the literal sense of the word.

"Am I correct in interpreting that you do this on a permanent basis?"

Dustin nodded. "This, and three different choirs at other churches in the area. Each group sings once a month."

"You have *four* youth choirs?" she clarified with a cough.

"My home church completely approves of my ministry," he said, sounding just a bit defensive. "I went through the vestry to get my marching orders."

"And I know you haven't told Addison about this," she repeated, a statement rather than a question.

"No," he said emphatically, his eyes widening as he realized where she was going with this. "And I'm not going to tell him now."

Two minutes ago she seemed to understand. Now she was pushing him again.

He bristled.

She touched his sleeve. "Why not?" she queried softly. "Surely if Addison knew of your work here, he would gladly release the trust fund to you. He would surely see this as I do. Dustin, this is not like your work with the homeless people. This is a legitimate ministry. You should at least consider the idea."

"No," Dustin snapped, his jaw tight.

He made eye contact with her and held the gaze, his green eyes flaming. "This ministry isn't about a trust fund. It's about me, the kids and God, and I plan to keep it that way."

He clenched his fists at his side. "Promise me, Isobel. Say you won't give me away."

Isobel couldn't move for a moment, couldn't breathe as she looked upon this strong, handsome, godly man who had so much to offer the world.

Finally, she broke the silence. "I promise, Dustin. Your secret is safe with me."

Isobel saw his shoulders and jaw relax at her words, and she relaxed a little bit herself.

"I knew you would understand," he said in a low, husky voice.

"And yet," Isobel said with sudden insight, narrowing her eyes warily on him, "this *is* about the trust fund, isn't it?"

He cleared his throat and pulled at his collar, even though he was only wearing a T-shirt. He shifted uncomfortably. "How do you mean?"

"I mean," she said firmly, taking his other hand and turning him toward her so she could look him right in the eye, "that you do not want the trust-fund money for yourself at all. Do you?"

He looked away from her gaze and shrugged noncommittally.

"Come clean, Dustin Fairfax," she ordered, using her hand to turn his chin back to her. "Admit the money is for the kids."

"So what if it is?" he growled, turning and walking away from her.

Isobel ground her teeth. Why was it so difficult to get any real information from him? He was like a mule when it came to his feelings. Sometimes she felt as if she were talking to a brick wall.

Stubborn man.

"For college," he said suddenly, turning back to her with a half smile on his face.

Isobel didn't say a word, waiting in anticipation for Dustin to continue.

His gaze showed the love and compassion he felt for the teenagers, as he clearly considered the words to explain what was in his heart.

"Some of the youth feel a call to ministry.

Others just want an education in a Christian environment. But private colleges are ridiculously expensive — way out of the reach of the most well-to-do student to whom I teach piano lessons. These kids are from this neighborhood. They would never get there on their own."

"I'm beginning to see where you're going with this," Isobel said, her excitement growing as love expanded in her chest.

"Scholarships," he finished. "I want to provide a way to help the kids get a much-needed lift in an otherwise menacing world."

"I still say you should tell your brother," she urged. "Surely if he knew —"

"No!" The subject was clearly and adamantly closed by the sheer tone of Dustin's voice. He stood taller, hovering over her. "You promised."

"I did. And I will keep that promise, Dustin," she vowed.

Suddenly he grinned at her, the light, buoyant smile that was classic Dustin. His smile alone was a tremendous relief.

"I haven't shown you everything yet," he said mysteriously.

When she smiled, he winked.

"Close your eyes," he said, taking her hand in both of his.

"Lead on," she said, closing her eyes as

he'd requested, relaxed and entirely trusting him to keep her safe.

Slowly, gently, he led her around several twists and turns until she had no idea in what part of the church she was. It smelled musty, like old wood.

" 'Kay, open," he said, sounding as excited as a little boy on Christmas morning. "See what you've been missing, Belle."

He emphasized his special nickname for her, chuckling with happiness.

They were in the belfry, the long thick ropes that led up to the big bell dangling directly in front of both of them.

"Are you ready?" he asked, leaning in toward her and stretching his arms until his hands met and clenched the ropes.

Isobel also clasped her hands around the ropes, but she could hardly concentrate on anything but being in the cradle of Dustin's arms. His musky western aftershave wafted around her and made her feel dizzy. His strong arms were tight around her; his warm breath tickled her neck when she turned.

She couldn't breathe and she couldn't move.

And suddenly she realized she didn't want to do either. She had no desire to move out of the comfort of his arms.

Ever.

"Ready?" he whispered close to her ear, and suddenly bells were ringing in Isobel's heart.

CHAPTER FOURTEEN

Isobel would never understand why people made such a fuss about Valentine's Day. Why make a special day to celebrate love? It only caused the majority of people to feel bad about themselves, and realize how alone they were in this world.

Not Isobel, of course.

She didn't buy into the commercials.

Well, okay, she usually splurged on a box of chocolates for herself. But chocolate was chocolate — a female ritual, right? So what if it happened to come in a heart-shaped box?

Only, this year Valentine's Day wasn't about a box of chocolate.

She had a date. Even though it technically wasn't a *real* date, she couldn't stop her mind from thinking about it.

Or rather, *him.*

The last six weeks had been a genuine eye-opener for her. She was sure she'd learned more from Dustin, her supposed student, than he could ever have learned from her in twice the time.

He had shown her the world, taught her to really look at people and not just their clothing. He had made her care.

Care about the homeless. Isobel had been to see Rosalinda twice on her own since that first day, and the old woman was beginning to trust her.

Care about low-income youth. The choir had stunned her and opened her eyes to issues she'd never before considered.

Care about *him.*

Oh, but she was in trouble.

Because even though her own feelings were beginning to manifest in her heart and crystallize in her mind, she was terrified even to consider if Dustin might feel the same way about her.

There was no use pretending any different.

Talk about heartbreak.

From the beginning, Dustin had been the epitome of a gentleman in every way. She'd never met a man like him. He even opened doors for her.

But that was Dustin.

A true gentleman.

Yet there was nothing personal about that.

He would, she was sure, be just as polite to any woman of his acquaintance.

Her thoughts drifted back to the kiss they'd shared, but she didn't dare put stock in it. She'd been wrong before, associating physical affection with emotional strings.

Worse, at least in the long run, was that he hadn't made many changes in their six weeks together.

In fact, she wasn't positive he had taken to change at all, she thought, her mind sweeping over the events that had taken place at the John Elway Foundation benefit — and before and since, for that matter.

The Elway benefit had been sort of a midterm test for him, and he had blown it big-time. They had talked about it afterward — or rather, she had lectured. But what difference did it really make?

This was one of the major reasons she was standing on Dustin's doorstep at noon, when Addison's fundraising function wasn't until eight at night.

Or at least that's what she told herself as an excuse for the truth.

The fact that she knew this was their last day together, and she wanted to spend as much time as possible with Dustin, might have something to do with it.

But she wasn't about to admit it.

Her throat tightened. She was a professional, and Dustin was a business transaction.

She would not let herself cry.

At least not until she was back in the safety of her own condo.

Dustin opened the door on the first knock, surprising her. It was almost as if he'd been waiting for her arrival, which was impossible since she'd indicated she would show up closer to five o'clock.

"Hey, there, Belle," he greeted heartily and affectionately.

Isobel smiled at him, but her heart dropped like a stone tossed in the ocean. She was going to miss him so much the pain was indescribable.

For a moment she considered, as she stepped into the foyer and shed her jacket into Dustin's ready hands, that perhaps this didn't have to be the last time she saw Dustin.

She'd had a job to do, and she'd done it. She would make certain Addison was impressed with her work no matter how much she had to torture Dustin into a tux.

She would corner Addison and remind him what a gifted brother he really had. Steer the trust-fund issue by emphasizing Dustin's stellar personality and gentle heart.

Surely Addison would hear — and had to know, deep down, anyway — the truth about his brother.

Dustin *would* get his trust-fund money. That objective had become all-important to her, now that she knew what the man was really like.

"You don't look surprised," she accused, putting her hands on her hips and staring up at him. "At my being early, I mean."

"I'm not," he stated, mimicking her movements. "As a matter of fact, I guessed you would make an appearance right about now. Actually, I wouldn't have been that surprised had you shown up at dawn."

Isobel was mortified and shot back, "Is that why you were standing at the door?"

He laughed. "What, you mean peeking through the peephole in anticipation of your arrival? I don't think so."

He closed the door and leaned his back on it.

"I'll go, then," she said, very aware of the way he casually blocked the door.

"Oh, no you don't. You're here, so now you have to wait and see the real reason I was so close to the door when you knocked."

"Oh, really," she said wryly, crossing her arms in defense of who knew what. "And what is this big mystery I should be aware of?"

Dustin's gaze swept across the floor and into the different rooms visible from the foyer. He appeared to be looking for something.

"What are you looking for?" Isobel asked at last.

"It's a she, not a what," he said vaguely, still looking around.

Isobel felt like she'd been shot in the heart, and not by Cupid's arrow, either.

Thick, green slimy jealousy oozed through her bloodstream as every nerve in her body quivered with this new information.

She?

He was chasing some woman around his house.

And he expected her to stand here and watch!

Who in the world was she, and more to the point, *where* was she?

Isobel had the sinking feeling Dustin was going to tell her something she really didn't want to know. She wanted to clap her hands over her ears like a child and wail, "La, la, la — I can't hear you!" at the top of her lungs.

Only her dignity saved her, and then just barely. She straightened her spine, tipped her chin and prepared for the worst.

For meeting the woman Dustin had apparently given his heart to, if the sweet, gentle sound of his voice when he talked about her was anything to go by.

"She's around here somewhere," he assured her, stepping away from the door and drawing her into the house with his hand at the small of her back.

Isobel allowed herself to be led, even when she felt like turning and running away.

"I can't wait for you to meet her," he continued, apparently, if the tender tone of his words was anything to go by, completely unaware of her stiff gait.

He led her to the living room and seated her on the couch. She couldn't help but feel a little jealous.

"She's pretty temperamental," he warned congenially, flashing Isobel a bright smile. "Hang on a minute and I'll see if I can find her."

Isobel sat straight-backed on the edge of the sofa, her hands brought up and clasped — not clenched — in her lap.

Composure, she coached herself.

She would maintain her dignity and refinement no matter who Dustin brought through that door. No matter how beautiful or poised that *woman* was.

She could be poised, too.

Please, God, let her maintain her poise.

And then Dustin appeared in the doorway and she screamed as if the house had caught fire.

Dustin nearly lost his footing, not to mention his surprise, as he scrambled to cover at least one ear against her racket.

She'd never been so surprised in her life, and she couldn't contain the joy flowing through her.

So much for dignity and refinement.

The fluffy little white kitten Dustin was holding in his arms stole her heart with its first tiny mew and one look into its luminescent blue eyes.

"I know you own your condo, Belle, but I didn't have time to check into your covenants before I got her. She was sort of an impulse purchase, but I couldn't seem to help myself."

He reached forward, offering the tiny, adorable fur ball out to her, and she instantly clasped it to her. "One of these *homeless* things, was it?" she teased.

He laughed.

"Is a kitty okay where you live?" His expression was an adorable mixture of excitement and anxiety.

He was almost as cute as the cat.

"Dustin," Isobel said, her throat tight.

She was half in shock as the kitten purred and pushed at her with its tiny paws, trying to find the most suitable position for a nap.

She'd never in her life taken to an animal as she did that little kitten. Her heart was swirling around in her chest — and not just because of the cat. Dustin's worried look was enough to make any sane woman forget to breathe.

She didn't say anything, enjoying the kitten and the small, innocent thrill of torturing Dustin a moment or two longer.

At length, he groaned. "I did the wrong thing again. I'm sorry."

"Dustin," she murmured, fairly at a loss for words but suddenly needing to comfort him.

"I was at the Humane Society yesterday," he explained in a gravelly voice. "I saw this little kitty and it reminded me so much of you, Belle. She's fancy, but she's also a real cutie."

Stroking the soft fur of the now comfortable cat, Isobel laughed and said, "Don't tell me. Let me guess. You volunteer at the shelter in your *spare* time."

She was pleased to see a little color darken his face. He shrugged and chuckled. "You caught me."

"Is there anything you don't do?" she teased, smiling and winking at him.

"Shoulder massages," he quipped merrily. "But I could work on that. In fact, I really think I should."

So saying, he moved behind the sofa and began working the knots out of Isobel's shoulders. His strong hands were soft and tender, a real paradox, but one she didn't wish to ponder at the moment.

She hadn't realized how tense she'd been until Dustin's gentle touch unwound her tight, tired muscles and she started to relax.

"The weight of the world shouldn't be on these delicate shoulders of yours," he said huskily, his warm voice close to her ear.

She sighed. "I know what you mean. It feels like it sometimes, though. I think I take life too seriously most of the time."

She'd never admitted that to anyone, but Dustin's kind ministrations were having a funny effect on her brain — and her tongue.

She found herself telling Dustin things she'd never told another living soul, not even Camille. She quietly admitted what it was really like living with a bitter mother and no father at all.

She told him how she always wondered if she was the reason her father had left, and not for another woman, as her mother had said. Isobel always wondered if her mother resented her, though of course she'd never shown it in any way.

But she would always wonder why her father had never come back.

She told him how badly she wanted to get away from Texas — to do more, *be* more, than most of the people in the small high-school class she'd graduated with, the majority of whom were still working on the family farm.

Just like the movies, right? Farm girl makes good in the big city.

Except it wasn't good — or at least not as good as she'd thought it would be. The same hollowness in her heart followed her everywhere.

Dustin just focused on her, asking quiet questions once in a while and letting her know with verbal assents that he was listening.

All the while he kneaded her shoulders and neck, thinking he might at least be able to help with some of the physical tension, even if he was not able to reach the emotional pain she carried.

A deep, gut-wrenching pain chewed at him all the while.

He didn't just want to commiserate.

He wanted to fix her problems.

Suddenly Isobel glanced at the digital clock on the end table next to the sofa and clapped her hand over her mouth. Her face flamed with embarrassment as she realized just what she'd done.

"I've been talking nonstop for over thirty minutes, Dustin," she exclaimed. "Why didn't you tell me to shut up?"

He chuckled. "Because I like listening to you," he replied gently, slowly brushing his hand down the length of her sleek brown hair. "And I think you needed to talk about some of that stuff. It's not healthy to keep things like that inside."

She shifted away from him, standing with the kitten still curled in her arms. She stroked the purring fur ball slowly, petting all the way down her back and smoothing any ruffles in her soft coat.

"What shall I name her?" she asked quietly, for some reason suddenly shy to look at Dustin after all she had revealed. She kept her eyes on the cat.

She felt, rather than saw, him smile as he came around the couch and up behind her, gently placing his hands around her waist. This time, his touch didn't make her immediately stiffen, though the longer they stood there, the harder it became.

"You're going to keep her, then?" he asked

softly, close to her ear.

She fought the urge to tense at his nearness, wondering why he affected her so.

Her heart knew the answer without question, but she pushed the epiphany aside just as quickly as it arose in her mind.

"Snowball?" he suggested, reaching around to stroke underneath the kitten's small chin. "She's as white as new snow."

"She is," she agreed, holding the fluff ball in the air so she could see its bright, curious blue eyes. "But somehow I think she has another name, if only I can figure out what it is."

"Take your time," he said, giving her waist a squeeze. "There's no hurry to name her. You can keep her for a week or so and get to know her own little special personality."

And as soon as he had said the words, Isobel knew her cat's name.

Epiphany.

Dustin turned her around, took the cat in one arm and brought his other hand up to her cheek, stroking it gently as he petted the cat.

"That's a good name. I like it. Unusual, but I agree it fits her."

She gazed up at him and nodded.

"You're shaking," he said.

"Am I?" Her breath increased as she tried

to still whatever physical symptoms were giving away the uneasiness of her heart. "It's a little cold in here, I think. Maybe that's it."

He lifted an eyebrow.

"Well, maybe I'm nervous about tonight. I mean, it's a really big night for both of us. A lot is riding on our presentation, right?"

"Right," he parroted, sounding not the least bit convinced. But then, under his breath, he continued, "I hate tests."

He brushed the pad of his thumb across her cheekbone, his gaze warm and tender. Isobel never wanted the moment to end.

Her *moment* would end all too soon as it was. Tonight was it, and then *it* was over. She wanted to savor every second with him.

She looked up at him — more charming than she'd ever imagined possible with that kitten cradled in his arm.

Dustin stared back, transfixed. He brushed his hand gently through Isobel's hair, using the tips of his fingers to feel the softness.

"Your hair is so beautiful," he said huskily. "It picks up all the highlights of the sun."

Emotion washed fiercely through her and she knew she was shaking.

But as his hand returned to her face, she realized he was shaking, too.

She plucked the kitten from his grasp,

knowing subconsciously they were both using the poor cat as a pawn, and moved to the safety of the opposite side of the room from Dustin.

She couldn't be next to him right now. She couldn't control the emotion — the *love* — flowing through her.

When had this happened?

She was going to do or say something really stupid and ruin the event for him — more than the evening, but the opportunity to win his trust fund.

Panic surged through her in nauseating waves. What was she to do?

Dustin stood across the room from her, his arms relaxed at his sides, his gaze on her.

He looked calm.

Handsome.

Perfect, in his faded jeans and plain black T-shirt.

She wouldn't change a thing.

What on earth was happening to her?

"Can I keep Epiphany here at your house until after the banquet?" she asked, surprised that her voice worked at all.

He looked down at the kitten, and then grinned up at her. "Absolutely."

She couldn't help thinking that tonight, when she picked up Epiphany, Dustin probably wouldn't be around much longer.

And she wondered if he was thinking the same thing. His gaze was suddenly pensive, his lips tight as their gazes met.

She wondered if they could part as friends. She hoped as much with all her heart.

Yet she had been hired to do one specific job, and that task would come to total fruition this evening at the banquet.

Dustin was ready.

They had been practicing every spare second, had discussed scenarios to make him appear more of what Addison was looking for.

He was going to wow more than his brother with his newly refined looks and manners. He would confidently present himself to his brother and receive the trust fund that was his due.

Dustin would be everything his brother hoped for, and more. She knew in her heart he wasn't going to blow it this time.

And then . . .

And then he would be nothing but a memory, out of her life forever.

Chapter Fifteen

Dustin fidgeted for the umpteenth time in as many minutes. He hated having a shirt buttoned clear up to his neck. He felt like he was choking, but resisted the urge to pull at his collar, an effort that was sure to be superfluous.

His red cummerbund was tight around his waist and made his back itch.

His whole outfit was bothering him. But right now, his mind was mostly on Isobel.

His heart pounded in anticipation of seeing Isobel — in a gown, jeans or otherwise. As far as he was concerned, she looked great in jeans and a T-shirt.

She looked great in every kind of clothing. How could a man ask for more than that?

In his book, clothes didn't make the woman.

Her *heart* did.

He'd never met a woman like Isobel, and

he wasn't foolish enough to think he ever would again. She was one of a kind.

A keeper.

Somehow, he had to find a way to keep her in his life.

A quick rap on the door pulled him abruptly from his thoughts.

Scooping Epiphany into his arms — and wondering briefly why Isobel had named the fur ball Epiphany in the first place — he opened the door.

The vision standing on the other side of the door was beyond words.

His breath swooshed out of his lungs in a rush. He dropped his arms slack to his sides, his mouth gaping — he hoped not too wide. The kitten made a mew of protest and gingerly hopped to the carpet.

He barely noticed her scurry away, tail held high in exasperation.

Dustin's gaze was riveted on Isobel, whose flowing red cocktail dress was gently blowing in the breeze, making the ruffles at the edges of the dress, just over her knees, stir and rustle like leaves in autumn. The red material made the brown in her eyes look like rich, dark chocolate, and she was gleaming with happiness.

He couldn't take his eyes off her.

"Dustin?" she asked, her light, twinkling

voice sounding hesitant.

"Mmm," he answered, not exactly a question. It was more that he couldn't form coherent words at the moment.

She shifted uncomfortably, losing her smile to a shaky, pinched mouth. She stayed on the porch even after he opened the screen and gestured her in.

"Say something," she pleaded, her voice now noticeably high and squeaky.

"Stunning," he said hoarsely. "Radiant. Electrifying. Stupefying."

Well, he'd got the last part right, anyway.

Stupid, stupid, stupid.

Now that he'd finally gotten his voice back he couldn't seem to shut up.

She brushed past him. "Thank you. I think."

He grinned inanely and turned as she walked by, his gaze still glued to her beautiful dress.

And smile.

And hair.

She looked him over, from the tip of his spit-shined black patent leather shoes to the top of his carefully groomed hair. Then she grabbed his arms and turned him around.

Once.

Twice.

Finally, she turned him back toward her

and reached up to adjust his bow tie.

"There," she said with a satisfied grin. "Now you, also, look stupefying."

She flashed him a cheeky grin just like the one he was so fond of giving her. "And all those other things."

He roared with laughter and wrapped his arms around her small waist, lifting her up as if she were a feather and spinning her round and round until she begged for him to put her down.

When he set her back on her feet, he couldn't help but brush a kiss across her soft cheek.

She blanched and looked panicked for a moment, then pushed away from him with her palms against his chest and moved well into the room, away from him.

His throat closed until he thought he would choke.

Was his touch so repulsive to her? Had he misread the signals of all the time they'd spent together, that she would be so uncomfortable in his arms, or being kissed by him?

This wasn't at all how he wanted this evening to start, and his own panic drove him back to her side, determined not to let that one action set the course for their evening together.

He wouldn't let this night be the end for

them. Somehow, some way, he had to convince her of his love, and that they were meant to be together for the rest of their lives.

Isobel had regained some of her color, but she still looked wary around him. It made him want to scream at the top of his lungs, he was so frustrated.

"So I pass muster?" he asked instead, giving her as playful a wink as he could manage.

She swallowed hard enough for him to notice. "Yes, sir, you do."

"May I suggest, then," he said in the smooth tone of a complete gentleman, "that we depart for the party immediately? I'm sure we're expected as soon as humanly possible."

"You *are* the guest of honor."

He offered his arm, but he didn't expect her to take it. "Shall we?"

"Thank you," she said with quiet dignity, and then looped her hand through his arm.

He led her to the door and opened it for her. He felt as if he was sweating like a pig, and hoped it didn't show. He did hope, however, that his first surprise of the evening would show, and quick.

"Oh, Dustin!" Isobel exclaimed as they stepped out onto the porch. "I can't believe you did this. It's so — not you."

"Yes, Isobel," he agreed wryly, "but it is very much you. Do you like it?"

"Like it?" she parroted. "Dustin, I'm absolutely thrilled to be taking a limousine to the party. We'll make such a splash! It's brilliant. Whatever made you think of it?" Her glistening wide-eyed gaze met his.

He laughed. "You did, of course. Do you want the truth? I was thinking back to our first conversation. Do you remember?"

She hovered one white-gloved hand over her mouth and chuckled. "Oh, I do. There was something about a sports car, as I recall. You wanted to give me a zippy ride around downtown Denver."

He lifted his chin and sniffed his offense at her remark. "It *is* a sports car, thank you very much. I've worked hard on it."

"Maybe, but it's still an old piece of junk," she teased merrily, apparently having forgotten her earlier problems. "I'm surprised it works at all. I'd be *afraid* to ride in it."

"Then I'll be sure to make you take a ride sometime, just out of spite." He grinned. "Do you remember how we talked about how snooty limousines could be? And here I am splurging on one."

She met his warm gaze and held it. "Thank you for this special, once-in-a-lifetime treat. Snooty or not, you're making me feel like royalty."

"Then follow me, my dear, beautiful princess. Your coach is waiting."

"Will it turn into a pumpkin at midnight?" she queried mischievously.

"Eleven o'clock. I couldn't rent the thing all night, you know. What do you think I am, a millionaire with money hanging out his pockets?"

"I certainly hope you don't have anything hanging out your pockets," she replied. "It's very unfashionable — unless it's a handker-chief."

Dustin patted his chest. "I've got that, and it even matches my bow tie."

"Impressive. Very impressive," she said with a chuckle.

The driver of the limousine parked at the curb, got out and opened the door for them. He was snappy and well-dressed in his uniform, and he gave them both a friendly smile.

Dustin helped Isobel inside, sliding close onto the seat next to her, though there was a lot of extra seat space in the vehicle.

Holding his breath, he reached his arm up and around her shoulders, where he settled with nonchalant ease, almost like a teenager on his first date at a movie theater.

He thought she might object to the close quarters, but she beamed up at him, her eyes glazed over with pleasure.

It made his heart turn over.

He cleared his throat. How could one look make his head spin until he wasn't sure he could think at all, much less speak?

"I special-ordered drinks for us for the trip over to the hotel." Somehow he got the words through his tight throat and dry mouth.

She looked at him as if he'd grown horns. "What?" she chirped.

He raised an eyebrow, perplexed.

She likewise raised an eyebrow at him, and suddenly he laughed.

"I didn't mean *drinks,* Belle, I meant *drinks.*"

He smiled and tipped the end of her nose with his finger. "I meant *real* drinks. You know — iced tea. Orange juice. Soda."

"Water?" she asked, her gaze again gleaming.

"Ice-cold, refreshing water. Only the best for you."

She smiled. "Please."

He opened the minifridge and twisted the top on a cold bottle of mountain spring water from Colorado, then opened a bottle of orange juice for himself.

With a big smile, he held up his bottle and indicated a toast. She grinned back at him and held her bottle aloft as well.

"To my princess. May every day be a fairy tale for you," he said in a husky voice.

"To my adventurer," she replied. "May tonight be the beginning of your dreams."

They tapped bottles and then both took a sip, their gazes locked on each other. Slowly they put their bottles down, but for a long while neither of them said a word.

It was a comfortable silence, but the electricity in the air felt sizzling, at least to Dustin. He wondered if she noticed the static buzz.

Finally, Isobel broke the silence, coughing softly before she spoke.

"Are you nervous?" she asked, taking a sip of her water.

"Me?" he responded, doing his best at sounding surprised by her question, though in truth what he was really trying to do was hide the nervous tension he felt sitting so close to her.

"Nah. I don't get nervous." He waved her question away with his hand.

She stared at him a moment, looking pensive. He didn't know whether she believed him or not until she shook her head and spoke. "No, you really wouldn't be, would you?"

"You sound jealous," he teased. "Don't tell me the phenomenal image consultant Isobel Buckley is afraid her greatest work won't pan out."

"Of course not," she said, sounding at once mortally offended and yet unsure of herself. It was a charming combination.

"I won't let you down," he vowed, his voice low and serious. His gaze met hers, pleading with her to believe in his strength — in *God's* strength. "You've done too much work on me for me to fail you now."

"Dustin," she said, turning every bit as serious as he was, and making him feel immediately uneasy, "I want to tell you something. It's really important to me that you hear me out on this."

She reached out and pulled his chin toward her so their eyes would meet. "Oh, what a nice, smooth shave," she said in surprise, rubbing her hand along his cheek and jaw.

"Huh? Oh, yeah. I went out of the way for you this time. I shaved twice today. It gives a new meaning to clean-shaven." He chuckled.

"You look nice," she said softly, sweetly and almost hesitantly.

He looked her straight in the eye as he

spoke. "Thank you."

"Be that as it may," she continued as if he hadn't spoken at all, "I want you to know something about tonight."

She sounded incredibly earnest and resolute, so he didn't throw a wisecrack at her this time.

"Go ahead," he urged.

"I think you look absolutely perfect. I think the things you do — known and unknown — more than account for making a contribution to society.

"In short, I think you've made progress in every area I was hired to work with you on."

"Thank you."

"Maybe you aren't taking my meaning," she prodded, though in truth Dustin thought he knew exactly what she was getting at. He supposed he didn't want her to go there, though it looked as if he had no choice in the matter, as she was pursuing it anyway.

He nodded and stared into her chocolate-brown eyes, feeling as if he could get lost in them. His arm around her shoulder tightened territorially.

"It may be," she said slowly, obviously carefully selecting her words, "that your brother will not agree with my assessment of your progress up to this point."

She took a deep breath. "I cannot fathom how that could happen, Dustin, but nevertheless, it is an eventuality we should think about and prepare for, in case the worst-case scenario becomes a reality."

"Believe me," he said gruffly, "that's almost all I ever think about anymore. That stupid trust fund. I hate it." He knew his annoyance showed in his voice, but he couldn't help it.

He didn't want to obsess over money, even if it was for a good cause. He hated that his father had done this to him, and yet here he was, on his way to *the* banquet.

"In short," she continued, interrupting his thoughts, "you might not get that money, Dustin. Addison may deny you your trust fund. You may have gone through all this agony for nothing."

"Agony?" he repeated dumbly, wondering what she was talking about.

He didn't remember any pain at all.

He remembered the way Isobel swished her long brown hair when she was irritated.

He remembered how her eyes glowed when she was happy.

He remembered the sweet, high tone of her laughter.

Was that agony?

Maybe, in a way, it was. It sure produced

turmoil in the general area of his heart.

"It's okay," he said gruffly, squeezing her shoulder to show his support. "I'm fully prepared for the contingency you mentioned." He laughed, but it was an empty sound. "This is my family we're talking about, and I, better than anyone, know what they're capable of."

He paused, thrust his fingers several times through his once carefully combed curls, and said, "I love my brother, and I know he loves me. Whatever happens, happens."

"I think you do." She reached up to stroke the backs of her fingers across his cheek. The soothing movement calmed him a little.

He paused, embracing the emotion that was enveloping him completely. He struggled to gain control.

"Addison is the only family I have. No matter what the outcome of the trust fund, he is my brother — and my brother in Christ." His throat grew tighter at every word he spoke.

Isobel cuddled into his arm and laid her head upon his shoulder. His head swirled with emotion as he tightened his embrace around her.

He wanted to feel this way for his entire life. He wanted to take care of Isobel, to hold her and protect her in his arms.

And most of all, to love her forever.

"I wish I had a brother or a sister," she said wistfully, squeezing his arm. "All I have left is my mother."

"But she's moving out here to Denver, right?" he asked, stroking her arm. "To be with you? See her grandkids?" he teased.

Isobel laughed. "Well, maybe someday. About the grandkids, I mean."

She took a deep breath. "Mom will be moving up next month, if the weather permits and she can close on her house. I've found a nice apartment for her here in one of the retirement centers.

"She likes the idea, and it will be nice to have her around. Sometimes a girl just needs her mother's advice — even if that girl happens to be approaching thirty."

She curled into him, as if seeking his warmth. It felt wonderful to him, and he pulled her in closer next to him.

Isobel sighed quietly. "You know, Dustin, I'm still working through my issues with my father. I don't think he was a good man. Not at all.

"And of course I will never be able to rid myself of the guilt, always wondering if it was me."

He groaned softly in agreement. "I know what you mean."

Oh, how he wanted to be a shield around Isobel, protecting her from the kind of pain she had experienced with her father. It made him angry that anyone could treat her with anything but respect and love.

"I'm getting through it, though," Isobel continued. "With God's help, I am."

She paused, catching and holding his gaze, though he wanted to look elsewhere.

"Forgiveness is a powerful thing, Dustin. I long for the day when that tremendous weight will be lifted from me for good. When I can finally forgive my father for all he has done — and not done — for me."

Dustin stiffened. "You've only told me a little bit about what your life was like as a child, but I can imagine the rest. What he did to you is unforgivable. It won't be easy to let go of." His voice was low and fierce.

"No. It won't be easy, Dustin. Not at all. In fact, I think it will be the hardest thing I will ever do," she said sincerely.

"And yet . . ." Dustin said, his voice laced with anger and frustration.

Already an idea was forming in his mind. What had really happened to Isobel's father? Something just didn't add up.

Isobel continued, breaking into his thoughts. "What my father did was unforgettable, but not unforgivable. God is not the author of *forgive and forget,* though I think we often get confused by that."

She paused until Dustin looked her way. "God only asks us to forgive."

He frowned and creased his forehead, thinking of his own father, of the situation he was now in because of that man. "I don't know. I just don't think I'm up to that sort of thing. You have more grace than I."

"Oh, Dustin," she implored.

"I could never forgive my father," he said vehemently. "Not ever."

CHAPTER SIXTEEN

He would have said more, but the limousine came to a stop at the hotel, and the driver opened the door to allow their departure.

Dustin stepped from the car and offered a hand to Isobel, thinking that as bad as his tuxedo was, it must be that much more difficult to wear a gown.

He was glad he was a man. Especially with Isobel on his arm.

Isobel took his hand as they approached the hotel, unconsciously lacing her fingers with his. She didn't even notice until he smiled softly and squeezed her hand.

Apparently he didn't mind.

She was quite disturbed by their conversation in the car. Dustin was carrying around as huge a burden as she, and her heart yearned to help free him from it, to help his pain go away, even if she could not relieve her own.

If only he could believe her words.

What her father had done still hurt her, and it still came to mind from time to time. That was only human nature.

Anger and distress had lessened from those memories as the years had gone on. God had relieved her of some of that pain, made her realize that no matter what had happened, it was still within the realm of God's reach, and though she hadn't known it at the time, He had taken care of her, carried her through the difficulties and on to a newer, better life in Christ.

If only Dustin could see what she saw, could know what she knew.

It would be a start.

She was shaken from her thoughts the moment they entered the hotel. Camille hailed her in a loud and boisterous voice.

"Isobel! Dustin! I've been watching for you for like — forever!"

Isobel laughed. "I imagine you have. Have the festivities started?"

Camille smiled at her friend. "Only just. And of course it won't really get off the ground until the guests of honor arrive."

"Oh, don't call us that," Dustin said with a loud groan. "I'd really rather be a wallflower than the life of the party. Or at least this once I would."

Isobel raised her eyebrow at him. The man

who could and did talk to everyone without the least discomfort now wanted to be invisible?

"I do," he insisted.

Isobel squeezed his hand. "I'm afraid that's just not possible this one time, Dustin. No matter how much you wish it."

Camille's gaze dropped to their linked hands, and she smiled widely and winked at Isobel, then made a funny face indicating that she was aware that they were entering as a couple.

Isobel flushed with embarrassment, and then realized she didn't care what Camille thought. She was proud to be with Dustin, and it wasn't something she wanted to be embarrassed about.

Dustin pulled at his collar with his free hand, yanking it around as if trying to find a comfortable place to breathe.

"So then, Camille, can you point us in the right direction?" he said in a scratchy voice.

"Certainly," she said, using all her charm on Dustin, who didn't appear to notice Camille at all. He only had eyes for Isobel, and for tonight, she was going to enjoy it.

"I think you'll find the surroundings familiar," Camille continued, "although admittedly the atmosphere has changed substantially."

"I beg your pardon?" Dustin asked, looking adorably confused.

Camille grinned at both of them, her smile like that of a cat. "Oh, surely you remember. Fifth floor? Ring any bells?"

Isobel and Dustin looked at each other and broke into laughter.

"You know," Dustin said as they entered the glass elevator, "I really dislike heights. Especially glass elevators."

Isobel laughed, shaking her head at his obvious distress. "Why didn't you tell me? We could have taken the stairs."

He pointed at her two-inch heels. "In these outfits? We wouldn't make it up one flight of stairs, much less five. Can you imagine what Addison would say if we didn't show up because we were stuck in a stairwell?"

By then the elevator had reached the fifth floor. Isobel chuckled as Dustin stepped out and planted his feet firmly on the floor.

"It's good being on dry land again," he said, theatrically wiping his brow. "I'm so incredibly relieved. I can't even begin to tell you, Belle."

"Ha!" Isobel replied. "You think you're sweating now. Just wait until we walk in there."

She pointed to the open double doors,

behind which was Dustin's one opportunity to make or break his chance at his trust fund.

Dustin scowled for a moment, sizing up the open doors, which to Isobel looked very much like a mouth — a whale's mouth, perhaps, or a tiger's.

Suddenly Dustin shrugged and grinned. "No time like the present," he said, offering his arm. "Would the lady care to accompany me to my doom?"

She curtsied playfully before taking his arm. "I'm absolutely honored to be with you under any set of circumstances."

Oh, how true her words were.

If Dustin only knew the truth.

As soon as they walked into the ballroom, they were met by Addison, along with many friends and acquaintances they both knew.

Isobel recognized many prominent faces in the room, people who would gladly give generously to a cause such as the Children's Hospital cancer ward, which Addison had picked as his charity of choice for the evening. This would be a good night for the hospital.

She was glad for that.

"Welcome, Isobel," Addison said, politely shaking her hand and giving her a friendly smile, which she returned in spades.

Then he turned to Dustin, his expression giving nothing away as he looked his brother over from head to foot.

Isobel realized suddenly that Dustin had never fixed his hair from when he'd run his fingers through it. His curls were showing.

She held her breath.

"Hello there, Addy boy," Dustin said at last, shifting from foot to foot.

Addison hesitated a minute, just staring at his brother. Then he suddenly stepped forward, smiled broadly and threw his arms around Dustin. "It's good to see you, bro."

Isobel's eyes moistened with tears, and as she met Dustin's gaze, she thought she saw a telltale gleam there, as well.

She smiled and stepped aside as Dustin animatedly returned the bear hug, giving back what his big brother had offered.

"You two look great," Addison said huskily as he moved back and dropped his arms. "Feel free to mingle around the ballroom and enjoy the food."

Addison turned to her. "Isobel, your friend Camille picked the caterer, and let me tell you, the hors d'oeuvres are spectacular, and that says nothing of the meal she has planned."

"Camille has a gift for these things," Isobel said with a laugh.

Addison waved his hand at Dustin. "From what I can see, Isobel, you have a gift, too. I've never seen my baby brother look so spiffy."

Isobel's heart raced. Did this mean Addison approved of what had been done and saw beyond the obvious — that Dustin would get the money in his trust fund?

She could only hope.

But she was also aware that this might not be the last test of the evening. Dustin would have to continue to be on his best behavior, and he might be called upon to disclose a little more than he was comfortable with.

Dustin once again offered her his arm, and they moved deeper into the room, talking to various friends and colleagues, and making general conversation with those they did not know.

Dustin leaned down close to her ear. "This place looks so familiar," he teased. "Although I have to say it does look a lot different tonight." He laughed. "I don't see a model's runway anywhere, thank goodness. Or any racks of clothes. Whew."

"It's more like the ballroom of a prince's castle," Isobel whispered, her head swirling as she looked at the red and gold decorations that had transformed the room so completely.

"I can assure you, Addison is no Prince Charming," Dustin said with a laugh.

Isobel looked up at him, her eyes wide and her heart in her throat. She thought if her heart swelled with any more love than she felt at that moment that she might simply burst.

"I wasn't thinking of Addison," she said quietly and tenderly.

Dustin's eyebrows immediately pinched together, as did his lips.

Isobel felt an urgent sense of panic.

She had said the wrong thing.

She was making an issue out of something that simply did not exist, at least on Dustin's part. When would she get that through her thick skull?

She immediately promised herself she would be more careful about what she said and how she acted around Dustin for the rest of the night.

She could not give her feelings away.

That would not be fair to Dustin. This was his night, and she was here to support him. She would not ruin a night he was sure to remember the rest of his life by throwing herself at him.

"Camille is a wonder with decorations," she said in a rush. "Like I said before, she's really gifted as a hotel manager."

"Yeah," said Dustin, sounding dazed and confused. "Gifted."

The announcement that dinner would be served saved Isobel from further embarrassment.

Ever the gentleman, Dustin once again offered his arm as they weaved their way around the tables looking for their place cards.

Dustin pulled at his collar for the hundredth time, stretching his neck to both sides in an apparent attempt to ease his anxiety, and perhaps to gasp a quick breath of air.

Every movement he made was apparent to Isobel, who felt his anxiety so strongly and fiercely it started to become her own.

He shifted in his jacket. "Where are we supposed to be sitting?" he asked in a strained voice. "I've got enough to think about without having to sit on the floor to eat."

She was certain he hadn't meant the words as a joke, as tense as he was, but though she tried to restrain it, she couldn't help herself.

She burst into laughter.

"No matter what you think your brother thinks of you, I doubt very seriously that he expects us to dine picnic style."

Dustin looked at her, his eyes glazed over as if he hadn't heard her at all.

"And if it is, hon," she said, still laughing, "I'm in a lot more of a pickle than you are. At least you're wearing trousers."

Dustin stared at her for a moment, the same glazed look in his eyes.

Suddenly, the clouds parted, the sun broke through and he smiled. The happy-go-lucky man she knew and loved appeared back in his eyes.

"Let's find Addison," he said. "Surely he knows where he seated us."

Dustin took her hand and led her to the head table nearest the raised platform. Addison was seated by a famous hockey player on one side and a well-known national politician on the other.

"It's about time you got here," Addison said, smiling at them. "I was about to feed your salad to my pet rabbit."

Dustin raised both eyebrows in surprise, but said nothing.

Isobel squeezed his hand.

"Well, sit already," Addison said, indicating the two vacant chairs opposite him. "I'm sure Isobel is hungry, even if you are not. It's really not very nice to keep your date away from the dining table, kid."

Dustin looked down at Isobel, panic in his eyes.

She knew what was bothering him. He had to sit at the lead table and act like fancy banquets were something he did every day.

"You can do this," Isobel whispered. "It's just food."

He nodded, a smile pulling slightly at the corner of his mouth. "Right. Just food. I'm hungry. How about you, Belle?"

He held the chair out for her to sit and then seated himself.

With a flair that surprised her, he selected the right fork and gently dived into his salad, taking slow, small bites.

As the courses changed, Dustin leaned toward her. "Smile," he whispered. "If you keep looking like that, everyone is going to know I'm a fraud."

"You're not a fraud," she whispered back fiercely.

Dustin spoke frequently throughout the meal. Unlike Isobel, who had to force herself to be outgoing for the sake of her business, Dustin was a people person. He got along with everyone, and made easy conversation that would have been painful for Isobel to initiate.

After the meal and before dessert was served, Addison rose and moved to the podium on the platform. He turned the microphone on and tested it, then looked down at Dustin and smiled.

"Tonight is an important evening," Addison announced to general applause.

"As you know, tonight's event was to sponsor the cancer ward at the Children's Hospital in Denver. My company, Security, Inc., has asked you all here to generously match our donation of five hundred thousand dollars."

The guests roared with approval, and it was several minutes before Addison could continue.

"I am astounded by the giving hearts in this community, and am proud to announce that not only did you match our contribution tonight, but you surpassed it. Our total tonight is one million, ten thousand dollars. I'm sure the hospital will be overwhelmingly grateful for your generosity."

Dustin whistled under his breath. "I had no idea my brother was doing such philanthropic things," he said to Isobel.

"Philanthropic or Christian?" she replied, meeting his gaze with her warm chocolate eyes blazing.

"You may have a point," he said.

"There is another reason we've gathered tonight," Addison continued, cutting off their conversation as Dustin gripped her hand.

"As many of you know, in my father's will, he left me in charge of my baby brother's trust fund, with very stringent conditions."

"Some baby brother," a man called out from a rear table.

"Point taken," Addison said with a laugh.

The crowd laughed along with him.

"Anyway, Father left strict instructions on distributing the fund to my brother, and I am happy to say that tonight I have witnessed a major change in him, exactly what I had hoped for."

Isobel became ruffled.

What did he mean Dustin had made a *major change?* He hadn't really changed at all, except for the tuxedo he was constantly fidgeting in.

"I'm proud tonight to introduce you to my brother, Dustin, and to present him with his well-earned trust fund."

Dustin's whole body was shaking. He gritted his teeth, trying to control his emotions. This was the moment he'd been waiting for, when he would finally receive his trust fund.

All he had to do was get his legs to work, walk up to the platform and receive the coveted check.

The only problem was that he was completely frozen to the spot.

He couldn't move a muscle, except to pull at his ridiculous collar and his strangling bow tie, which felt like it was getting tighter by the moment, choking him to death.

He certainly couldn't stand, never mind walk.

He took a deep breath, trying to steady his nerves and pull himself together.

Suddenly Isobel was out of her chair, standing behind Dustin with her hands on his shoulders.

He had no idea what she was up to, but he could feel her hands shaking.

"No," she said so loudly her voice echoed in the big room.

Addison cleared his throat and tapped his fingers against the podium. "I beg your pardon?"

"I said," she repeated, emphasizing each word as if she were speaking to children, "no."

CHAPTER SEVENTEEN

Panic rushed through Dustin.

What was Isobel doing? She was ruining everything they had worked for.

He could see the train wreck coming but he was helpless to stop it.

"Stand up," she whispered for Dustin's ears only, a command rather than a suggestion.

He complied, but only to turn and implore her with his gaze to stop whatever game she was playing and let things go as they were.

"Take it off," she said, once again in the loud, piercing voice that everyone could hear, even those clear across the room.

"What?" asked Dustin, in a daze.

"I said, take it off. Now."

He had no idea what she was talking about, so he stood staring at her, wondering if she'd gone completely mad from nerves or something.

"If you don't, Dustin, I'm going to," she

warned in a low voice.

"Ms. Buckley, may I ask what you are doing?" Addison asked from the podium. The rest of the crowd was so silent they could have heard a pin drop.

Isobel made good her threat, and finally Dustin understood what she was doing, besides killing any chance whatsoever he might have to get his hands on his trust fund.

She started with his coat, yanking it off his shoulders and down his sleeves until she'd completely shed it from him.

Then she started on his bow tie.

She stepped back and looked at him for a moment, then reached her hand up and mussed his hair.

Dustin felt a good deal more comfortable, which he supposed was a good thing, as he was going to his own funeral.

Isobel stomped up onto the platform, her high heels clicking with every step. Addison yielded the microphone to her without a word.

She paused and took a deep breath.

Dustin was holding his breath, half terrified and half oddly interested in what she would say.

After a moment, she pointed at him.

He cringed and wondered if he ought to

crawl underneath the table.

"This man, ladies and gentlemen, is Mr. Dustin Fairfax."

There was complete silence in the room as Isobel continued to point.

"I am a professional image consultant. Six weeks ago I was hired by Addison Fairfax to make over Dustin, to help him become something that would fit the terms of their father's will."

Dustin clenched his fists, unable to fathom what was going on.

"I admit I like the new haircut," she said wryly, and the crowd chuckled along with her. "However, I cannot let this farce continue. I am here tonight to tell you emphatically that Dustin has *not* made a major change that suddenly makes him worthy of the trust fund."

Dustin groaned quietly, seeing the end in sight. He could almost hear the chop of the ax.

"Dustin is not a person who likes to dress up and attend social functions," she continued. "He is most comfortable in faded blue jeans, old tennis shoes and a plain old T-shirt.

"He is more comfortable with his jacket off — it confines his shoulders — and his tie removed. Oh, and the buttons. Dustin does not like anything too tight around his neck."

"Ms. Buckley," Addison whispered frantically, urgency in his tone.

She held up her hand to him.

"Dustin has not changed," she repeated, looking out into the crowd, "because, ladies and gentlemen, he does not need to change."

Several murmurs broke out among the crowd as Isobel's speech began to make sense.

"Dustin Fairfax is the most honest, giving, hardworking man I know. He makes all kinds of contributions to society, and we don't need to know what they are. As the Bible says, he keeps his good works a secret, so that his reward is in heaven.

"Dustin is the best man I know. He should get the trust fund simply because he completely deserves it. He has earned my respect, my confidence and my loyalty."

As she finished, she lowered her head, tears in her eyes.

The crowd was roaring with applause, many standing in ovation to her speech.

Addison quickly moved to Isobel's side and put his arm around her, whispering gently into her ear.

Dustin was on his feet in a second. Something about seeing his brother with his arm around Isobel spurred him to action like nothing else could.

He was gone in a moment.

"Do you know where we're going?" Camille asked, excitement lining her voice as she turned a corner in the clunky, boxy old car Isobel had never been able to convince her to part with.

Isobel leaned against the cool window and groaned, holding her forehead in one hand. "I thought you said it was a surprise."

Camille gave her a quick glance and smiled despite her friend's obvious agony. "It is a surprise. I just wondered — you know — if you recognized the neighborhood or something."

Isobel gritted her teeth. She didn't recognize the neighborhood because she wasn't watching where they were going.

She couldn't care less.

It had been three weeks since the banquet, three weeks since she'd seen Dustin, and she was miserable.

Addison had announced that Dustin would be receiving his trust fund, though he'd been gone by the time she'd finished her ill-fated speech.

She wondered if he knew he was getting his money.

Addison had given her a check, but she'd handed it right back, donating it to the Children's Hospital, the night's chosen charity.

It had felt like blood money.

"Oh, will you cheer up, already?" Camille chirped. "This is going to be fun."

Isobel begged to differ. Nothing was ever going to be fun again. In every man she saw Dustin's face, every voice, his voice. Every laugh, his laugh.

She wasn't sure if she would ever laugh again. The logical part of her argued that Dustin was a phone call away. She knew where he lived, for pity's sake.

But if he didn't want her, she wasn't going to go chasing him around, making a nuisance of herself.

And he obviously didn't want her.

It wasn't just that she didn't want to walk out of his life and never see him again.

It was that she wanted to be with him. She wanted to share every joy, every sorrow. *For richer and for poorer, in sickness and in health,* her mind mocked her.

How had she only now figured out what must have been obvious for at least a couple of weeks, maybe since the first day, when

Dustin walked into the deli with that awful haircut?

She was completely and unconditionally in love with Dustin Fairfax.

She had had relationships with other men before, but they had all been short-term and, in hindsight, rather shallow.

Stupid. Stupid. Stupid.

"We're here," Camille said, turning off the car. "Get out."

Isobel recognized where they were the moment she slammed the car door shut.

The church with the belfry and red doors.

She tried to pull on the door handle, but she had locked the door by habit when she'd exited.

"Camille, take me home. Now," she ordered, pulling on her friend's elbow.

She just laughed. "No way. Come on, girlfriend. Your future awaits you."

Then why did she feel as if she were going to a funeral?

She knew Dustin was waiting inside. She just didn't know why. And after three weeks?

She looped her arm through Camille's, and her friend patted her hand for good measure.

"Deep, slow breathing," Camille advised. "You can do this."

Camille had watched her mope about for

271

three weeks. She knew the agony of unrequited love herself. Why was she drawing this out?

Camille was in cahoots with Dustin, that's what it was.

Then they were inside, and the real surprises were only beginning to show themselves.

The youths were there, milling about and chattering up a storm.

Dustin was at the piano. He appeared not to notice her appearance.

But then the tune changed, and suddenly the choir assembled, humming a background to an unsung melody. Addison stepped from one side of the church, her mother from the other. They were both smiling.

She was confused.

Stunned.

Elated.

In a moment she was in front of the piano, and Dustin was seated at the keyboard. His kind, flashing green eyes were on her as he stroked his fingers lightly over the ivories.

His expression was as serious as Isobel had ever seen — his brow furrowed and his lips tight.

"Hey there, Belle," he said as if they had seen each other yesterday. "How's it going?"

"I — uh," she stammered, unable to process what was going on.

She cleared her throat and looked around her. "Okay, I guess."

He nodded gravely. "Well, I —" he started and then paused, his gaze locking on hers. "I'm feeling absolutely terrific tonight."

He smiled just for her. "No, better than terrific. Fantastic. Wonderful. I can't put it into words, how I'm feeling right now."

He put his hand on his heart, still holding his earnest gaze with hers.

She tried to hold back her grin but couldn't.

"Stupefying?" she suggested, knowing her eyes were gleaming with the hilarity of the private joke.

"Mmm, yes. I was thinking more along the lines of *supercalifragilisticexpialidocious.* You know, the word you use when you can't think of a word?"

Isobel couldn't help it.

She laughed.

He smiled gently. "Well, Belle, do you remember the night of the Elway Foundation benefit?"

"Ha!" she said, letting out a puff of breath. "Do I remember it? As I recall, it was your midterm, and you flunked."

He nodded and winked at the crowd

hovering around them and chuckling at the scene. "This is true," he said with a casual shrug of his shoulders. "I definitely didn't rank up to par."

"That's the understatement of the year," Isobel mumbled under her breath.

"Yes, well, anyway, I'm sure you recall that I was late that night."

"Very late."

"Very late," he agreed.

He paused for a moment, running his tongue across his bottom lip and looking deep in thought.

"I had a reason for being late that day, although I didn't tell you then what it was."

She was baffled. "Why not?"

"It wasn't finished yet."

"I'm sorry," she said, her forehead creasing as she tried to comprehend his words. "I don't think I understand. What wasn't finished?"

He looked at her then, long and hard, and yet tenderly. His expression was serious, but a soft smile quickly appeared.

"This," he said in almost a whisper.

Then his fingers ran over the ivories one more time, and he began playing the softest, sweetest song Isobel had ever heard.

She closed her eyes, reveling in the beauty of the music, and in the knowledge that

Dustin had written this song.

It was so beautiful, and from the way he had phrased it, she was certain it was the first song he'd ever composed on his own.

But why hadn't he simply told her that?

Did he think she wouldn't understand?

She did understand.

She understood Dustin almost better than she knew herself. She felt inexplicably linked to him, but she knew that this was only her side of a relationship that would never be.

Suddenly, Dustin began to sing, his clear, rich baritone piercing through the sanctuary even though he had no microphone.

And he was singing about her.

When Isobel heard her name, a finger ran up her spine and gooseflesh covered her arms.

The song was about her!

She gulped down and tried to pull in air, but nothing seemed to work. She felt as if she were suffocating.

His words whirled around her, every note burrowing into her.

He was singing a love song.

A love song!

Could it be that he returned her affections, that he felt the same connection as she?

Was it true?

Dustin continued singing, but his gaze met hers, and in his eyes she could see all the love and affection and commitment that she felt for him.

He smiled and winked at her in that crazy, adorable Dustin way he had, and her heart flipped over, and then over again.

He loved her!

Oh, how she wanted to be alone with him right now, to finally express all the feelings she'd kept hidden in the depths of her heart.

Dustin finished his song, clearly spelling out his love for her — by name.

And the next minute he was beside her, holding her hand. She was unaware of the crowd gathering closer to see what would happen.

She could only see Dustin, and the love beaming from his eyes.

Part of her screamed that it was too good to be true; that there was no way her dream could be becoming a reality.

And yet there Dustin stood, softly smiling just for her.

"This took me longer than it should have, Belle," he said, dropping her hand and putting both his hands in his pants pockets.

"For what?" she asked breathlessly.

"To figure out I'm in love with you."

Her breath rushed out of her body and she stood like a statue, his words having frozen her.

"And there was one more thing."

"What?" she whispered, all choked up.

"Your father."

"My *what?*" she screeched.

Her mother put her arm around her.

"Mom?" she asked.

"This should come from me," she said.

"What?" Isobel didn't know whether to be happy or sad — but she was confused.

Dustin answered. "Before I could make things right with you, Belle, for all you did for me, I needed to find out what happened to your father. I wanted to give that knowledge to you as a gift — so we could go forward with a clean slate."

"So you went to my mother?" Isobel demanded, adding a bit of anger to the cloud of emotion she was feeling.

"Not immediately, no. First I hired a private investigator. When I found out the truth, I went to your mother for confirmation."

"What do you mean *confirmation?* Mother? You knew what happened to Dad? Why he didn't come back?"

"He did leave your mother for another woman," Dustin said gently, placing a hand on her mother's shoulder. "And he thought a clean break would be better, at first."

"But then that other woman broke it off," her mother offered, a tear sliding down her cheek. "Your father wanted to come back home again. I wouldn't let him."

Isobel was stunned into silence. Dustin put his arm around her.

"I was angry, Isobel," her mother explained. "Angry and hurt. And then —" She broke off suddenly, closing both hands over her face.

Dustin cleared his throat. "You were about five years old then, Belle. Your father, he was — he overdosed on medication. The police believe it was an accident."

Isobel burst into tears, and then, as if a light poured on her, she remembered the day her mother had gotten a certain telephone call, and what had come of that.

"Do you think . . . ?"

But she didn't have to finish the question. Dustin nodded. "I do think. And now you can let it all go."

Still crying, her mother embraced her. "I'm so sorry for not telling you the truth. I was so ashamed of my own behavior."

Isobel hugged her tight, and they cried together. The others, besides Dustin, stayed back, letting the family renew their own vows.

After a while, Isobel turned to Dustin. She opened her mouth to speak, to tell him she loved him, to thank him for his heartfelt consideration. But the words wouldn't form.

She couldn't breathe, much less speak.

He smiled gently and put a finger over her mouth.

There was no need for her to speak. The love between them was almost a tangible thing.

Suddenly he pulled his hand from his pocket, a white velvet box clutched in his hand.

She might have panicked, with all these people around her, watching her every move.

But the look in Dustin's eyes calmed her, and she waited to see what he would say.

He flipped open the box to reveal a lovely gold ring with interwoven aspen leaves made from genuine Black Hills gold.

Gently, carefully, he removed the ring and held it up to her.

"This is a promise ring, Isobel," he said in a soft, smooth baritone filled with the richness of his love for her.

"If you accept this ring, you are accepting my promise to you — before God — to love you, care for you, be there for you, and when the time is right, make you my wife."

She stared at him for a moment, just letting his words sink in.

How she loved this man!

Slowly and with great regard, she lifted her left hand and accepted the ring, which Dustin quickly slid onto her hand, as if she might change her mind.

This, she knew, she would never do. And she realized she owed Dustin the same kind of vow he had given her. He needed to hear it from her.

As he started to move his hand away, she grabbed it and held it.

"Dustin," she said, her voice choking with emotion, "I love you, too. I accept this ring, not only as a token of your love, but of my love for you.

"I will — before God — love you, care for you, and when the time is right, I will become your wife.

"I look forward to getting to know everything about you, and to bond our love by our time together."

"Kiss the woman," a man in the crowd called.

Soon, everyone in the crowd was calling for the culmination of such serious vows.

Dustin grinned like a cat, amusement

lighting his eyes. "What do you think, Belle?" he whispered for her ears only.

She grabbed the front of his shirt and pulled him to her, so their lips were mere inches apart.

"I think," she said with a sly smile, "that you'd better kiss me."

Dustin obliged willingly, closing the distance between them with a soft, sweet kiss.

"We're on it!" a man and a woman said. She thought it might be Addison and Camille, but she wasn't sure and she didn't really care.

A moment later, the bell was ringing, clear and loud inside the sanctuary of the church.

Around them, Isobel could hear applause.

She thought all the angels in heaven must be applauding at that moment, for the joy of a man and a woman who'd finally found each other.

CHAPTER EIGHTEEN

Four and a half months later

Isobel heard the pounding on the door to her condo, but she was busy playing with her cat, Epiphany, and didn't want to move to get it.

"Camille, can you get that for me?" she called.

Camille appeared at her side, dressed, but with a towel wrapped around her hair.

"In any other circumstances, Izzy. But I think you should answer it this time."

With a groan, Isobel picked herself up off the floor and went to the door.

Not a huge surprise, Dustin was on the other side of it. What did astonish her was the man standing behind Dustin.

His brother — Addison.

She hadn't seen Addison since that time at the church when she'd received her promise ring.

It was only then she realized Dustin was

holding a box with a ribbon — and it wasn't just any box, it was a clothes box.

She couldn't have been any more surprised. She felt as if he could knock her down with a feather.

"Come in," she said to the men, holding open the door. "Addison, it's great to see you."

He rubbed his hands together as if he were nervous, but then gave her the pearly-white Fairfax grin.

"You're looking as pretty as ever."

She smiled and shook her head at him.

She would have said more, but Dustin cleared his throat.

"Excuse me," he said wryly, "but isn't anyone interested in the gift I brought? The gift in the *clothes* box?"

She laughed. "You know I am."

He nodded. "Good," he said firmly. "Then you'll follow my directions to the letter."

She frowned at him, her eyebrows furrowing. Who had exchanged her sweet, carefree Dustin for a man who gave orders?

"It's important, Belle. Just do what I say, this once?" He was pleading with her now, his big green eyes like a puppy dog's. She couldn't resist.

"Okay, so what gives?" she said, giving in

with what she hoped was a modicum of dignity.

Camille had wandered out to the living room, and Isobel was surprised to see her hair was not only dried, but styled.

What was going on here?

Dustin handed her the box. "There are clothes in here," he said, as if it weren't obvious. "I want you to go in and change. You have to wear what's in the box today. Promise?"

She had a feeling this was a promise she was going to regret, but how could she say no with all these people staring at her?

"Camille can help you get dressed," Dustin suggested offhandedly.

As if she hadn't been dressing herself all her life?

But she smiled and took the box from Dustin, then allowed Camille to herd her into the bedroom.

"What did I just get myself into?" she said to Camille.

Her friend just laughed. "Why don't you just open the box and see?" she suggested merrily.

Isobel set the box on the bed, held her breath and untied the blue ribbon, gently easing the top off the box.

Blue jeans. It was blue jeans. *Faded* blue

jeans, to be exact.

It figured. It just figured.

"Well, put them on," Camille suggested with a wave of her hand. "You know he said you have to wear this outfit today."

"Yeah, don't remind me," she groaned.

She picked up the jeans and found an even worse surprise.

"Oh, it's a T-shirt," she said of the carefully folded cotton material. "He knows I hate T-shirts."

"Well, look on the bright side," said Camille. "At least it's hot pink. You'll look really cute."

"I'll look really grungy," Isobel replied, but she pulled the jeans over her hips.

"Okay, okay, the shirt," Camille urged.

"All right, already. Don't rush me. I'm not in a huge hurry here."

"Well, it's not fair to leave Dustin and Addison waiting," Camille advised.

Isobel picked up the hot pink T-shirt and rolled her eyes at her friend. "So I'll get dressed, already."

She pulled the T-shirt over her head. "I'm ready. Let's go."

Camille looked at her strangely. "O-kay," she said, drawing out the word. "You first."

Isobel shrugged. "Whatever."

She stepped out of the bedroom and back

into the living room to find both men smiling from ear to ear.

"Well?" asked Dustin, rubbing his hands together.

"Well, what?" she said, lifting her eyebrows.

Camille sighed loudly. "This woman cannot take a hint."

Isobel turned to her. "What are you talking about?"

Dustin laughed. "Come here," he said, leading her to a full-length mirror in the hallway. "Now, look at yourself."

She did, and then she screamed for joy, throwing her arms around Dustin and kissing him soundly.

Though the words were reversed in the mirror's image, she had still easily been able to read the words printed on her T-shirt.

Marry Me.

Dear Reader,

Change.

It's a six-letter word that draws fear in all of us, from the humblest to the mightiest.

We can't control many of the changes that happen to us — but sometimes we become obsessed with changing ourselves.

As Dustin and Isobel learned, and what Moses himself learned straight from God, maybe life — today's life — isn't about change at all. Maybe it's about being just who God made you — right here, right now.

God loves you just as you are, and has placed you just where you are — for a reason.

It's worth a thought.

I love to hear from my readers! You can write me at:

Deb Kastner
P.O. Box 481
Johnstown, CO 80534

Resting in His strength,

Deb Kastner

QUESTIONS FOR DISCUSSION

1. Dustin was willing to have himself made over in order to get his hands on his trust fund. How far would you be willing to go for a large sum of money? Why or why not?
2. Dustin was elusive and went out of his way to make sure Addison didn't discover many of his activities. Why do you think he did this? (Hint: Matthew 6:3)
3. Both Dustin and Isobel had gifts and abilities they shared with others in God's name. What gifts and abilities do you have that you could use to help others in any kind of need?
4. Isobel stuck with Dustin even when things got rough. How long should you stand the antics of a person who makes you uncomfortable before you say, "That's enough"?
5. Isobel felt abandoned by her father, who left without a word when she was a young child. If we are a child of God, are we ever

really abandoned?

6. At the end of the book, Dustin gives Isobel a promise ring. If he is sure, and she is sure, why do you think he didn't give her an engagement ring?

7. If God has blessed you with abundance in your life, in what ways can you think of to give back in your communities, nation and works?

8. If, like many of us, you live paycheck to paycheck, what ways can you think of to give back to God for His generosity in giving us His Son?

9. What do you think you would do if you suddenly came into a windfall of money? Be honest!

10. What is a tithe? Use a Bible concordance to look up verses to help you answer this question.

ABOUT THE AUTHOR

Deb Kastner is the wife of a Reformed Episcopal minister, so it was natural for her to find her niche in the Christian romance market. She enjoys tackling the issues of faith and trust within the context of a romance. Her characters range from upbeat and humorous to (her favorite) dark and brooding heroes. Her plots range widely from a playful romp to the deeply emotional.

When she's not writing, she enjoys spending time with her husband and three girls and, whenever she can manage, attending regional dinner theater and touring Broadway musicals.